Enticing

Written by:

Quisha Dynae

Copyright © 2021 by Quisha Dynae

All rights reserved. No parts of this book may be reproduced in any form without written permission from the publisher, except by a reviewer who may quote brief passages in a review to be printed in a newspaper or magazine.

Published in the United States of America

by Love Irene Publications

PO Box 481703

Charlotte NC 28269

This book is a work of fiction and any resemblance to persons, living or dead, or places, events or locales is purely coincidental. The characters are productions of the author's imagination and used fictitiously.

Chapter 1

Jenday Coley

I sighed as I lay in my bedroom staring at the ceiling in deep thought. I have so much on my plate, that at times, it gives me a headache. Just thinking about the massive amount of responsibility that was thrust upon me six years ago, has me stressed the hell out.

I am twenty-four-years-old, and I am supposed to be auditioning for Broadway right now, but instead, I am basically the guardian of my sixteen-year-old sister. I have been raising her since I was only eighteen years old, and she was just ten.

I was accepted into Julliard while I was attending, Northwest school of the Arts, but the day after my High School Graduation, my life took a drastic turn. I remember it like it was yesterday, the day that I had to give up my dreams.

"Baby girl, go sit your ass down somewhere." My father, Keith shouted at my ten-year-old sister, Leah. He was grumpy, which meant that he was in his room snorting coke, or whatever other drug he could get his hands on at that time. Keith wasn't worth shit. That was why my mother was always working. If she didn't, we wouldn't have a pot to piss in.

"You don't have to talk to her like that, Daddy," I said to him with the roll of my eyes. I wasn't trying to be disrespectful, but he didn't have to talk to her that way. He was grumpy, and had an attitude. He didn't like to be bothered when he was in his zone. My sister was too young to understand that though.

"You are grown now, Jenday. You can get the fuck out." His words slurred.

"Don't worry, I will be out of your hair at the end of Summer." I turned to walk away, pulling my little sister with me. We were headed to my bedroom when the phone rang. When I answered, a lady asked for my father. She stated that she was calling from Atrium Health Hospital, and that it was urgent.

It took me a minute, but I finally convinced my father to unlock his door. He snatched the phone from my hand, and spoke to the lady on the other end.

"What? No no no no no," he screamed. I didn't know what was wrong. His cries caused my little sister to rush into the room. I couldn't tell her what was going on because I didn't know myself. I just had a feeling that it was nothing good.

My father hung up the phone and stared at us with sympathy, and at the same time, he appeared heartbroken. His eyes were glossy, and tears were running down his face. It took a few minutes for him to calm down and speak to us. He told my sister and I to put our shoes on and he asked if I could drive us to the hospital.

"Is something wrong with my momma?" I asked him with tears about to spill over the rim of my eyes. That was the only thing that could make my father show emotions the way that he was in this moment

"Just...please Jenday." His voice had changed drastically from just a few minutes ago.

I didn't say another word. My sister and I got ready, and he handed me his keys before we walked out of the door.

When we arrived at the hospital, that's when shit went south. We were told that my mother, Sadie, was possibly in a deadly automobile accident and they needed my father to identify the body. He instructed my sister and I to wait in the waiting room while he headed downstairs. We sat down and I held my sister preparing for the worst. I prayed that it wasn't her, but in the back of my mind I knew it was. Why else would someone from the hospital have called us?

Our Dad didn't come back for thirty minutes, and when he did, I saw it all over his face that the person was indeed our mother. He sat us down right there in that waiting room and gave us the devastating news. My sister and I could not control our tears. We were heartbroken and didn't know what would happen to us without our mother. It wasn't like my father was a responsible adult.

After the funeral, that's when everything really went downhill. My father was going missing for days, and then weeks at a time. He wasn't taking care of us at all. We didn't have anyone else to take care of us. That's when I had to make the decision to decline the offer to Julliard.

That was the worse day of my life. My sister and I still live in my childhood home. Most of the time we are alone because my father stays in the streets. After my mom passed away, he went on a downward spiral. Worse than what he already was. He showed up at the house when he needed to bathe, or if he was hungry. He still had a key, and I wouldn't take that from him. He doesn't do normal crackhead behavior and steal things. I love my father, therefore, I wouldn't deny him entry to the home that he helped pay for at one point.

Our mother was hit by an eighteen-wheeler. The guy had been drinking. The crazy thing about it was, he was still alive. Barely had a scratch on him. He got sentenced to ten years for vehicular manslaughter. We were also awarded over a half of million dollars for the accident from the company that the guy drove for. I put most of that money up in a college fund for my sister. I then put two-hundred thousand in a savings account for a rainy day. The remainder, which was about seventy-five thousand was in my personal savings account. I still have most of it.

My sister receives a social security check from our mother that comes in my father's name. One thing I can say is that he has sense enough to sign the check over to me every month to help pay the mortgage. The check wasn't but so much, so I had to get a job so I wouldn't have to keep tapping into my savings account.

I started out working at the mall. That wasn't cutting it for me though. I still enjoyed dancing, therefore, I somewhat put it to use. I used to hit the club scene heavy. A local artist, Bizo, noticed me dancing and asked if I wanted to be in his video. From that point, more local artist began to contact me on my Instagram page. It wasn't Broadway, but I got paid for doing what I loved. I also dance at a gentleman's club. No, I am not a stripper per se. I am an exotic dancer. My shows are sensual, and sultry. I give an experience. The way that I fluidly move my body has those men emptying their pockets. The club was always packed when they knew I was doing a show. I don't socialize with anyone; I do what I have to do and get out of there.

Leah, my sister walked into my room and jumped on my bed. She lay down beside me and asked, "What's wrong sis, why you in here looking sad?"

"I'm not sad, I was just thinking. We are not going to worry about that though, what you want to do today?" I asked her. I try to spend as much time with her as possible to try and compensate for the loss of our mother, and the fact that our dad wasn't around consistently.

"I don't really have nothing in mind. Maybe we can order food and have a girl's day. I don't really feel like going anywhere. Have you heard from Dad lately?"

I sighed before telling her, "No, I have not. But you know he will show up when he needs too."

"Are we not enough?" Leah questioned with a saddened look on her face.

"What do you mean?" I questioned while turning in the bed to face her. I raised my hand removing a few of her short loc's out of her face. She just started her Loc journey six months ago.

"I mean, are we not enough for him to want to do right by us? You know, for him to get off drugs and come home to stay?"

I didn't like discussing things like this with my sister. Yes, she was sixteen-years-old and was old enough to understand what was going on, but I know it hurts her. She was a daddy's girl at one point, then our dad started hanging out later, and coming home high. I have no idea how he ended up on drugs. My mother told me that he was hanging around the wrong type of people after he got laid off from work. I guess not working was too much for him. Maybe he didn't feel like a man since he couldn't help with the bills. My mother even threatened to leave him at one point, and he still wouldn't lay off the drugs and shit.

"Leah, I'm sure it's not that. He loves us, but when that monkey is on your back, it's hard to get off. I would get him into a rehab program, but he would only take off like he did our mother all those years ago. When he gets tired, he will get himself clean. Hopefully, that will happen sooner than later. But don't think that he doesn't love us, okay?"

"Okay," she replied with downcast eyes.

"Come on, let's get up and head to the grocery store so we can cook. I don't want any restaurant food." Jenday stated as she stood up to get her day started.

I loved spending time with Leah. She was growing up fast, and she's also smart as hell. She doesn't give me a hard time at all. She cooks, and helps out around the house. I appreciate her for never making this hard for me. Leah is my best friend, and I am hers.

We walked through Super Wal-Mart placing any and everything into the shopping cart. We were standing on the bread aisle when I heard, "Got damn, baby."

I turned around seeing this fine ass man. He had almond colored skin and tattoos adorned his perfectly carved body. However, I wasn't interested. I already had too much on my plate. Plus, he was rude. I rolled my eyes at him and reached for the bread that we needed.

"Oh, it's like that?"

"Not interested," was my simple reply.

"Well fuck you too. You too beautiful to walk around with a nasty ass attitude. I bet if I put this dick in your life, you will straighten up."

Leah gasped at his words like she couldn't believe that was how men talk to women these days. My eyes were wide then I narrowed them at him. I placed my hand on my hip and said, "I know you see this child right here. You are being disrespectful which is why you wouldn't ever stand a chance with me." I rolled my eyes then told Leah to come on. I maneuvered the shopping cart around him and we went about our business.

"He was rude," said Leah.

"Yes he was. That's why I moved around. I don't have time for a relationship anyway," I let her know.

"But you deserve to be happy."

I glanced at my little sister and smiled before saying, "Raising you makes me happy." I placed my arm around her waist and pulled her into me. She smiled up at me as we continued to shop before checking out and heading home for our girls day.

Keifon Michaels

Damn, lil' baby was fine as fuck. Her skin was the color of a pinecone. Her loc's were the color of autumn leaves, and her body…oh my God, she was perfect. I can't get with that nasty ass attitude, though. It was best I let her ass go on about her business.

I continued to the aisle with beer and grabbed six cases for my exclusive gambling spot that I ran with my brother, Orion. We've had this spot for years with no problems. We make money with this shit too. You had to pay to play. Upon entry, there is a two-hundred-dollar cover charge. The spot was attached to our club, *Groovy Nights* . You couldn't get in from the outside, you had to come through the club. We have it that way for a reason. You only knew about our spot if you knew someone who was already in. You have to have a password to even get inside the door. In order to gamble, there was a thousand-dollar minimum. Only real ballers entered that door.

I paid for my items and then got in my black, big body Benz and headed to the spot to meet Orion so we can set up for the night.

It took me twenty minutes to pull up, and when I did, Orion was pulling up right beside me. I got out of my car opening the back door to get the beer out and Orion came over to help me.

"What's good bro?" He spoke and we slapped hands before lifting the beer and heading inside.

"Hey Keifon and Orion," Halle, one of the waitresses spoke sexily. Ol' girl was a trip. Both of us have fucked her. She thinks we don't know, but bro and I tell each other everything. Although we are close now, it wasn't always that way.

Orion is actually my stepbrother. My Mom, Iris, married his Dad, Jahamal, when I was thirteen, and he was twelve. We hated each other at first. I was missing my Dad, who got killed a year earlier. I didn't want a new Dad. Plus, we were both used to being the only child. We bumped heads off gate. I can't even count on one hand how many times we came to blows. At one point, my Mother expressed to his Father, that maybe it wasn't a good idea for them to get married. Jahamal wasn't having it though, and put his foot down. He loved my Mother so much that he was willing to do anything to salvage what they had.

One day he told us to come into the back yard when my Mother wasn't home. He knew that if she was home, she wouldn't go for what he was about to do. He told us that we were going to settle our issues that day. We were either going to fight each other until we got it all out, or we were going to fight him, get our asses beat, and still leave the shit alone. We chose the first option. Orion and I fought each other until we were tired with our lips busted and black eyes. If I remember correctly, we also had bruised ribs. Afterwards, we sat on that ground for an hour. His father wasn't going to let us get up until we talked our issues out. He went inside, and eventually, we talked it out.

I expressed to Orion how I felt they were taking my Mother away from me. Keep in mind we were only twelve, and thirteen. I was a spoiled ass lil' nigga. I wanted my mother to myself. We called a truce. Oh but when my mother got home and saw the state we were in, we bonded over my Mother cursing his Dad the fuck out.

However, we really didn't start getting close until we entered into our ninth, and tenth grade year of High school. We were both at a new school since our parents had just moved into a new house in the University area. My mom and I lived in the hood up until that point.

We were the new kids and they thought they could treat us any kind of way, especially Orion, he was a lil' skinny kid at the time. He was quiet and didn't bother anyone. These niggas started bullying him. I wasn't going for that shit. When I saw niggas jumping him in the bus parking lot, I ran and jumped right on in. It was four of them and we beat all those niggas asses. When the administrators broke it up, we were suspended for five days. We were grounded at home, but our parents took into account that I had his back. His father simply asked, "Did y'all win?" He wasn't as mad as my Mother and all he said was that we had to stay in the house. Ever since then, we have been thick as thieves.

"What's up, baby? You getting everything straight for tonight?" I asked Halle.

"Yea, it's all good. Things are straight," she replied.

"Ahhight, take these beers out and put them up. It should be a few more boxes in the back," I told her.

"Yea, I already handled those," she said before doing as I asked. When she turned around, Orion and I admired her fat ass. She was always dressed scantly trying to catch a nigga. She was a straight hoe and everybody knew it.

A few hours later, security showed up and started letting people in. It was a line outside to get in the club. Once in the club, folks lined up in the hallway to get next door to the gambling spot which we also had security at that door.

Orion and I made our rounds making sure things were straight around the club before making our way to the other side. The music was playing as drinks were being passed around.

"Yo, what's up, my boy," Bizo, a local rapper spoke to us while sitting at the blackjack table.

"What's good man, I see you winning good tonight?"

"Hell yea, but holla at me later, I got some shit to speak with y'all about." Bizo stated.

We agreed knowing that he wanted to speak about that other shit we into. On occasion, we get orders from a crime syndicate. They hired us to boost cars. At first, we were against it until we were approached by Bizo. He explained how easy it was and how much money he makes from it. He taught us how to disarm a car alarm and how to hot wire that shit. The first few times were rough with us almost getting caught, but we finally got it right. Shits easy.

"Keifon." I heard my name being called. I turned my head seeing Prissy. I fucks with her. We've been messing around for a year. We not exclusive or no shit like that. I bust down a few bitches here and there, but she easily became my main.

"What's up, Prissy?" I held out my arm and she walked into me giving my a tight hug. I leaned down pecking her neck before pulling away.

"You good, you need anything?"

"No, we good," she said speaking of her and her two friends that were standing behind her.

"Ahhight, let me know if y'all need anything," I replied.

"I need one thing." She smiled with her eyes moving to my waist.

I smiled and asked, "Oh yea, what's that?"

She stood on her toes whispering in my ear, "I want some dick."

"Oh word. Come on." I grabbed her hand and she told her friends that she would be back. I led her to my office and locked the door.

"Bend over," I stated and she did as I asked. I didn't bother with foreplay or none of that shit. I unbuckled my jeans, and pulled my mans out covering it with a condom. I swiftly entered her dripping pussy. I fucked her ass good before we made our way back to our people. The night went well. Niggas were loosing left and right. For everything that someone won, we took thirty percent of those winnings. We got rich off this shit, among other things.

We both have an associates degree in Business from Central Piedmont Community College. We didn't want to go off to school. Shit, we didn't want to go to school at all, but my Father made a deal with us. If we go to school, he would pay our rent until we were straight. So, that's what we did. We figured, two years would be a breeze, and it was.

Our parents knew what we did for a living; well most of it. Our Mother doesn't know about the cars, but our father does. Anyway, he explained the importance of having an education beyond high school since we were planning on owning businesses. Me and bro were good. We were living life and enjoying that shit.

As everyone was leaving, Bizo approached us to have a word. We led him to my office and closed the door.

"Yo, we have an order for a Range Rover, and a Porsche Panorama," Bizo stated.

"Ahhight, the Range will be easy. Them shits all around. But the Panorama, you don't see too many of them," Orion replied.

"Nah, I saw two of them shits after I got the order. I followed them. They both stay off Providence road, so that ain't no thang."

"Oh word? Well lets get it then. When you tryna do this?" Orion questioned.

"Whitin a week?" Bizo told us.

"Let us know when you ready. We got this. I'm about to get out of here, though. A nigga tired as fuck," I said.

"I feel you. Aye, before you go. I have a video shoot for my new single coming up. I was wondering if I can use your club. You know I'll pay."

"It ain't no thang. You can get it. Don't even worry about the money. As long as you film before we open the doors for the night, you good," Orion let him know.

"Cool, 'Preciate that." We all stood and slapped hands with Bizo before leaving out.

Orion and I made sure everyone was gone, before locking up. This has been a long day, and my shower and bed are calling my name.

Oba Ibrahim

"Incoming," someone shouted as an ambulance came to a sudden stop at the emergency entrance of, Novant Health downtown, where I worked as a nurse practitioner. I love my job. Some of these patients make my day; the pleasant ones anyway. However, when someone gives me a hard time, I completely understand. When someone is in pain, anything can come out of their mouths. I am a patient person, though.

"I got it. What happened?"

"Car accident. His vitals are stable. His femur in his right leg is broken," the paramedic passed along the information.

"Ahhhh, this shit hurts." The man yelled out.

"We are going to take care of you, sir. What is your name?"

"Frank."

"Okay, Frank. I got you. Take him to bay three." They pushed him to the bay and I began my initial assessment. His femur was definitely broken.

"Frank, I am going to contact the surgeon on call. Your femur is indeed broken. We have to get that repaired. Hold tight for me, okay?"

"Okay." He closed his eyes fighting through the pain.

Twenty minutes later, he was pushed to the operating room. My job with him was done. It is five o'clock in the morning and almost time for me to clock out. I have an hour left. I made a few more rounds in the ER assisting with patients. When six o'clock hit, I was out of there.

The first thing I did when I walked into my home was take a shower. As soon as my head hit the pillow, I was out. I had the next three days off, and was in need of some rest.

******

My phone rang waking me out of my sleep. I was sleeping good, too. Whomever it is, will have to call me later. Right after I hit decline, they called right back. I groaned as I answered without looking at the caller id.

"Hello."

"What's up, baby? You still sleep?" My friend guy, Tommy asked. He's not really my boyfriend, we've just been messing around for nine months. He's not really my type, he is just cool peoples. He's respectful and treats me right. He owns a Marketing firm, and the fact that he is so handsome makes it easy to keep him around.

"You know I just got off not to long ago, Tommy," I replied.

"Babe, its three o'clock."

My head popped up as I looked at the time on my phone. However, I laid back down, not like I had something to do today.

"Damn, I didn't even realize it was that late. What you up too?"

"Shit, I wanted to spend time with you today? You up for it, I know you just came off your four days."

"Yea, we can get up later." I sat up swinging my legs over the bed standing up before heading into the bathroom to take care of my morning hygiene.

"That's what's up. I'm pulling up," he stated causing me to sigh. I didn't want him over here this damn early. The one thing I didn't like about this man was that he's too damn clingy. He wants to spend all my spare time with me. My sister, Dola, told me that he has the potential to be a psycho. I always laughed it off, but she might be on to something. But until he shows actual signs, I'll keep him around.

"Okay, I'm coming." I hung up the phone and washed my hands before going downstairs to answer the door.

"Hey Oba." He engulfed me in a hug. I hugged him back with a smile before placing a kiss to his lips.

"Your morning been good?" I asked.

"Yes, it's better now that I see your thick ass." He squeezed my booty before pulling away. I turned and walked into the kitchen to fix me something to eat.

"I'm about to make me an omelet, you want one?"

"Yea, I can eat." He sat at the island and watched as I prepared our food.

I sat his bacon, cheese, onion, and spinach omelet in front of him. I then poured us some orange juice, and sat beside him with my food.

"Damn, I didn't realize I was this damn hungry." Tommy stated as he scarfed down the food like he haven't eaten in a few days. I frowned watching him. He was finish with his food before I even finished with half of mine.

"I see, slow down before you choke," I chuckled.

"My bad baby. I'm just so damn hungry." He slowed down a bit and we enjoyed our meal.

"Oba, how do you feel about us moving in together. I mean, we've been at this thing for a minute." He lifted his glass taking a sip of his orange juice.

"Uhm, I don't think that will be a good idea, Tommy. We aren't even together. That's a little extreme don't you think?" I cocked my head to the side waiting on his reply.

"No I don't. What exactly are we doing then?"

I sighed placing my fork down. I don't know what he was thinking. This shit is coming out of nowhere. We have never talked about being exclusive before. If I'm being completely honest, I only wanted a fuck buddy. I'm not one to sleep around, so that is his purpose in my life. If I would have known that he couldn't keep his feelings in check, I would have moved around to the next man.

"We are enjoying each others company." I shrugged my shoulders watching a frown appear on his face.

He was silent for a while as he took the last sip of his juice. He then turned towards me as he chewed and swallowed his food before asking, "You don't see yourself with me, Oba? I mean, I'm really feeling you. You are beautiful, have a good head on your shoulders. You're independent and your sex is bomb. I can see myself with you, but if you don't feel the same, I don't see the point." He gazed intently at me. I don't know what type of answer he wanted, but I told the truth; sort of.

"Right now, I'm not looking for exclusivity. At this point in my life, I'm just having fun."

He scoffed as he questioned, "In other words, I've been wasting my time? For real, Oba?" His voice raised a few octaves which I didn't appreciate.

"How were you wasting your time? We chill, we fuck, we go out sometimes, what more do you want from me?"

He got off the stool, turning mines around so that he was standing between my legs and said, "I want you to be my woman. You're a good catch." He leaned in pecking my lips a few times.

My answer wasn't changing though. I told him, "I appreciate the compliments, but what I said stands. I'm not ready for a relationship. For one, I'm too damn busy for one."

"Maaan…" He raked his hand down his handsome face as he stated, "You are a grown ass woman. People make time for what they want to make time for. If I'm wasting my time, let me know and I'll move around."

"What?" I jerked my head back. His voice elevated again as he replied, "I don't have time for this shit. I am a grown as man. If I want a fuck buddy, I'll go out and get one."

"Do what you gotta do." I rolled my eyes.

"You serious right now?" He took a step back glaring at me.

I nodded my head in response. He chuckled and replied, "If I leave, I'm not coming back. I will find a lady that's worth my damn time."

"Okay." I don't know if he thought I would change my mind with his threat or what, but he was mistaken. I didn't care if he left or not.

"You something else, Oba. I can't believe this shit right now. I could have been with a woman who is appreciative of my time."

"Tommy, at this point, whatever you're saying doesn't matter. You can go ahead and get out my damn house." I stepped down from the stool and began to clear the counter. I rinsed the dishes off placing them in the dishwasher. He was still standing there glaring at me. I guess he thought I was going to change my mind.

I turned around and asked, "Why you still here?"

"Man, fuck you Oba. You ain't shit."

"I'll be that. Now get the fuck out," I hollered.

"Bitch, who the fuck you talking to?" He stalked towards me. We were so close that I felt his breath at the top of my head.

"Back you, Tommy." I tilted my head up to see his face. What I saw caused my body to tremble. He was angry and I was afraid at this point.

"Go on now. Get out my damn face." I screamed.

In a millisecond, he had his hands wrapped around my throat.

"Fuck you bitch! After all the shit I did for you, this how you do me? Me! I am a good man!"

I struggled to get his hands from around my neck. He gripped it tighter the more I tried to loosen his grip.

"St…stop." Tears sprang to my eyes. My vision blurred as I became lightheaded. I felt around the counter gripping the knife that I used to cut up the onions. I swung it but he jumped back letting me go. I began to cough to catch my breath.

"Ge…get the…fuck out. I never want to see you again." Tears were streaming down my face as I held the knife up silently threatening him. His ass was crazy just like my sister said. He glared at me for a few more seconds before saying, "Fuck this." And walked out of the house leaving my door wide open.

I let out an excruciating cry as I made my way over to shut and lock the door. I rubbed my neck because it was still burning. I can't believe he did all of this because I didn't want to be in a relationship. I can't imagine how life would be if I would have agreed to live with him. Thank God I dodged that bullet.

Orion Russell

"Yo, Pops," I hollered as I stepped out my car. He was outside pulling the trashcans to the front of the house to be picked up tomorrow morning.

"What's up, Son?"

"Ain't shit. Just came to check on y'all." We shared a hand slap and hug.

"You know you don't have to check up on us. We good."

"Oh, I know, but still wanted to stop by. Did momma cook?"

I started calling, Iris, mom when I was younger. My Mother left to follow her dreams and travel the world. She said being a mother was too much. I use to be upset about it, but fuck that bitch. If she didn't want us, then the hell with her. I mean, who the hell gets pregnant purposely then decides it's not what they want. That's some backwards ass shit. She may as well not even agreed to have a baby with my Pops. Then again a nigga wouldn't be in this world. Me and my Pops were good though. He was an excellent Father. He raised a good ass man. I may be into some shit, but that doesn't mean he didn't raise me right.

My Pops met Iris, and our lives became better once Keifon and I started getting along. I wouldn't change shit that has happened in my life for the world.

She loves me just like I was her biological son, and the same with Keifon and my Pops.

"She in their cooking now," he replied.

"Ahhight, let me go holla at her." I walked past him into the house going straight to the kitchen.

"Hey, Ma." I wrapped my arms tightly around her kissing her cheek.

"Hey, baby."

"What you in here cooking? Shit smells good." I rubbed my stomach.

"Just frying some chicken wings with rice, and brussel sprouts."

"I know I get a plate, right?"

"Of course, I'm going to feed my baby." She smiled that beautiful smile of hers.

"Thank you, Ma."

"What he in here begging for, Iris?" Jahamal made his way to her. He leaned down to meet her short five-foot-five-inch frame and pecked her lips.

"He's just hungry, Jahamal," she replied as she turned the stove off.

"You don't have to feed this nigga, sweetheart."

"Leave my baby alone. If he's hungry, I am going to feed him."

"Iris, you do know he's a grown ass man, right? Talking about your baby. I'm your only damn baby." He kissed her jaw. My mother rolled her eyes as she replied, "I have three babies. Y'all go on and sit down. Keifon should be back in a minute and we can eat. My Pops and I did as my mother asked.

"How's business, son?"

"You know how it is. We stay making that paper," I replied.

"Good, good. And that other thing?" He whispered letting me know he was talking about us stealing cars.

"We only do that shit when we're needed. It isn't often. We have a job in a few days though."

"I hope y'all being careful out there. It's dangerous. You know I use to do that shit back on the day."

"Yea I know. But you've been on the straight and narrow. We wouldn't dare get you involved." My Pops had his own security firm. That's where the security that we hire for the club comes from.

"I hear you, son."

I heard Keifon speaking to my mother. Within seconds, they were both walking into the dining room with dishes. Shit smelled so damn good, and I am starving.

"What's up Pops and Orion?"

"Hey son."

"What's good bro?" I replied. We all held hands as my Pops said grace.

"Father God, in the name of Jesus. Bless this food and the hands that prepared it. Bless my wife and children and cover them daily. In the name of Jesus, Amen."

"Amen," we all repeated.

Our mother is a Godly woman. Our Pops goes to church with her, but he isn't as strict. He will still curse you out, and beat your ass, then turn around and ask for forgiveness.

We enjoyed our meal before Keifon and I said our goodbye's and left.

"Where you headed?" Keifon asked me.

"Shit, headed to the crib. Krysta coming through."

"Oh ahhight. I'll holla at you then." We slapped hands, got in our cars, and left.

I pulled up to my two-story home in Matthews. I love staying out here away from everybody. I have an apartment in the University area too when I don't want to drive all the way home, or when I am entertaining a lady that I don't want to know where I live.

When I pulled up, Krysta was already in my driveway. She stepped out of her car as soon as I pulled inside my garage. I waited for her to enter the garage before pulling her into a hug. We exchanged pleasantries before I pressed the button on the wall to close the garage door, then led her into my house.

She knew what she was over here for, so their was no need for too much talking. We headed to my bedroom and got right to it. I was tired as fuck. After she came twice, and I bust a nut, I sent her on her way.

Chapter 2

Jenday
One week later

I had a video shoot with Bizo today. He gave me the address to the club they were meeting at. The dancers and I have been rehearsing for the past five days. We had the routine down packed by now.

Leah wanted to tag along and I had no problems with that. I grabbed my duffle bag with my outfits and headed towards the door.

"Come on, Leah," I hollered out.

"Coming," she shouted. She appeared in the living room and we left out headed to, *Groovy Nights*.

******

We pulled up to the club seeing a line of expensive cars. It was a lot of men and women standing around. A line was around the building as security searched the extras before letting them inside the club. The camera operators were setting up their expensive equipment.

"Dang, it's a lot of people out here," Leah stated as she swiveled her body around taking in the scene.

"Sure is, come on so I can start getting ready." We made our way to the front of the line.

"Hey, I'm one of the dancers."

The security guard's eyes moved down my body before replying, "Ahhight, go on in."

We made our way through the door and I spotted Bizo immediately standing in the DJ booth. He had a microphone in his hand as he gave instructions to the extras.

"Aye, I just need y'all to turn up when my song plays. That's it. Y'all can handle that right?"

Everybody shouted, "Yes." He gave the mic back to the DJ before he stepped out of the booth and headed towards me.

"What's good, Jenday." He reached in for a hug.

"Hey, you remember my sister Leah?"

"Yea, what's up, baby girl."

"Hey," Leah responded shyly.

"Where are we getting dressed?" I asked.

The other dancers are upstairs in the corner office," he told me. I then made my way upstairs to prepare myself.

"Hey y'all."

"Hey Jenday."

"Oh good, you're here." The girls replied.

A make-up artist was set up in the corner working on one of the girls. I pulled Leah to the side of the room as I opened my duffle bag pulling out my outfit. We were wearing black two-piece outfits. The bottoms were high waist biker like shorts, with a bra that had rhinestones on them. I pulled out a pair of black pumps sitting them on the desk. I then got undressed pulling my outfit on. I handed Leah my shimmering body butter to apply to my back while I sat down applying it to the rest of my body.

"Can you put my loc's in a messy bun?"

"Sure. You look so pretty, sis." She admired me before doing my hair as I asked.

"Thank you."

My sister was my number one fan. She often told me how proud of me she was. It meant a lot coming from her. It's times when she has to stay home alone for me to work, but she knew it was necessary for me to take care of her. Leah is a good kid. She is an exceptional student, and doesn't give me a hard time. She doesn't ask me for much, but anytime she does, I make it a point to get it for her. For instance, she has a shoe fetish. I keep her laced in the latest Jordans, and Air Max's. She had more sneakers than I have heels.

"Okay, does it look right?"

I stood making my way to the mirror. I did a three-sixty in the mirror admiring my look.

"It's perfect, hun," I let her know. The other ladies were finish getting their make-up done, so I sat in the chair next while Leah helped the other five ladies apply their shimmer.

"Okay ladies, we are starting in thirty minutes. We are on a time limit. We have to finish before the club opens." We acknowledged, Bizo's manager before she left out the office.

"Y'all ready for this?" I asked.

"Hell yea," I heard a reply. I held auditions to choose these ladies myself. They were some of the best dancers in town. One of them came from Atlanta to audition, and she was the bomb.

My make-up was flawless. I was ready to do this. I was getting paid two-thousand dollars for this job. The other ladies didn't get paid as much. I only got this much because I held auditions and choreographed the routine, plus, Bizo was fond of me.

"Alright ladies, let's get out there. Leah, you can stand in the crowd if you want."

"Okay." She replied as I led the ladies out of the office, and headed outside where the first shots were going to take place.

This shot was only going to be with us, and Bizo's crew. Everyone else was inside the club waiting on the second half of the song. Then we will end it back outside. We all got in position waiting for the music to start. I stood beside Bizo with my hand on my hip. As soon as the beat dropped, my body began to move. We were winding our bodies, and thrusting our hips as Bizo rapped his lyrics. This beat hit hard too, I felt it all through my body.

Ooo, baby so thick, got me grabbing on that shit...

He made a motion like he was smacking my ass. I looked back at Bizo before winking my eye. It took two takes for everything to be perfect.

"Ahhight, cut. Lets move into the building." The video director stated. We all took a sip of water before getting into position on the dance floor. The extras were standing around, some with cups in their hands. We then started recording.

As I was dancing, I felt eyes on me. I searched the crowd while doing our routine. Then I spotted him. The guy from the grocery store. His eyes were on me hard as he salivated at the mouth. I wanted to roll my eyes so bad, but I didn't want the camera to catch it.

I noticed him lick those thick ass lips of his. He was fine now. Dark skin, with a low cut and a beard lining his face. He was tall as hell, at least six feet four inches. He was dressed simply in a pair of denim shorts and a white T, with white, and red Jordan 12's on his feet. Yea, he was sexy and he knew it. I could just tell he was conceded as hell.

My eyes moved to my sister. She was moving to the beat having a good ass time. I noticed the camera move to her, and she was taking it all in. She could dance too, she learned from the best of course. I moved through the club and ended up beside ol' boy. He was cheesing hard as hell as he took me in head to toe.

One of our moves caused for us to dance on someone, and since he was right there I had no choice. I turned so that my back was facing him and dipped my body while looking back at him. I bent down touching my toes before rolling my body up sexily. He smacked my ass and surprisingly, it turned me on causing me to put on a show. After all, it was good for the cameras. It looked organic. I turned facing him and dipped down popping my ass before coming back up and then landing in a split. I spun around bending my knees and got up bending at the waist so my ass was on him.

"Got damn," I heard him whisper. I smirked as the dancers then moved back to the middle of the dance floor and we finished the shoot behind Bizo and his hype man.

"And cut…"

"Good job, Jenday. You the shit, girl." Bizo stated.

I smiled brightly as I replied, "Thank you." I then turned to the ladies and said, "Come on y'all. Job well done." We made our way back to the office. I just slipped on my tights and left in search of Leah.

I spotted her talking to dude from the store. My face was in a frown as I hurriedly made my way to them. He had no business talking to her.

"You looked awesome, sissy."

"Thank you," I hugged her before asking, "What's this?" I pointed between the two.

"Oh, this is Keifon, we weren't really talking about anything. He was just saying how he remembered me from the grocery store with you. He was just giving you your props on your moves. I told him you were my amazingly talented sister." Leah smiled, but I didn't. She noticed my mood right away and her smile dropped.

"Did I…" She was about to ask a question, but he interrupted her.

"Hey, pretty lady. Let's try this again if you don't mind. My name is Keifon." He proffered his hand and I glared at it before my eyes moved back to his. His smile was beautiful. He had perfect white teeth that I have never seen on a man. He was a handsome man. Reluctantly, I reached out rolling my eyes saying, "Jenday."

"Jenday…that's different. Sexy ass name to fit a sexy ass woman." His tongue moved across his bottom lip, and my orbs followed it. I cleared my throat before saying, "Nice to meet you, I guess. Now my sister and I have to go." I grabbed my sisters hand preparing to walk away, but he gently placed his hand on my elbow saying, "Hold up, I'm just trying to converse with you for a moment."

"I'm sorry, but I'm…" I was in the process of saying until I heard, "Hey baby. Who is this?" A pretty woman placed her arm around his waist glaring at me through narrowed eyes.

Keifon smacked his lips as he stared down at her. It was like they were communicating with their eyes. She stood there for a few seconds before smacking her lips and stomping away.

"Now, like I was saying…"

"Nah, you wasn't saying shit. I can already see now, you have too much going on for me. Go on over there and talk to that girl because if she keeps giving me the evil eye, I'm going to walk over there and smack the shit out of her. Come on, Leah." His mouth was hanging open slightly as I walked away with Leah on my tail. He had some nerve tryna holla at me when he had some sort of situation on his hands.

When I was about to walk out the door, I looked back seeing Keifon having a few words with the chick, and it didn't look friendly. I didn't know what was going on with them. Even though it seemed like a fuck buddy situation, I didn't have time for it.

"Jenday, did I do something wrong?" Leah turned towards me when we got in the car.

"No, boo. I just know his kind. He is no good. We don't need to associate ourselves with men like him."

"What kind of man is that, because he seemed nice."

"Seemed, is the keyword in that sentence. Always remember that looks can be deceiving. By the way that girl walked up, and he dismissed her told it all. He's willing to be with her on his terms, and if he did that to her, I can imagine what he'll do to me."

She simply nodded her head in understanding as I drove us home. I was tired and was in need of a good hot shower, and my bed.

Keifon

I watched as Jenday's sexy ass made her way out of the building. Those damn colorful loc's added to her sex appeal. Prissy made her way back over to me asking, "Who the fuck was that?"

"Prissy, you are not my damn woman, and you don't have the right to question me about shit," I seethed. She probably done fucked up my chance with Jenday. I had to get her ass in my life. I'm not sure what her position would be, but I was willing to follow her lead if given the chance.

I heard Prissy smack her looks as I saw Jenday glance back at me and shake her head. Yea, I messed up already. I chuckled because she didn't know me too well. I had to holla at Bizo. If she was a dancer in his video, then he probably knew some personal shit about her.

"Keifon, you wrong for that. You don't be saying that when we be fucking?"

"That don't mean shit, baby. You giving me boyfriend privileges without me being your man. That's your fault. We have our fun, and you were cool with that."

"I still am." She looked off to the side.

"Well stop bitching and get wit' it. If you see me in my zone hollering at a female, move around."

Her face dropped as she had a saddened look on her face. I knew she would agree. Her ass did anything that I suggested. She didn't want to lose out on this good dick, or the bread I throw her from time to time funding her expensive ass life. She had her own money, she was a phlebotomist working at a doctor's office downtown. However, she loved spending my money, which I was fine with as long as I got the pussy when I wanted it.

I pulled her into a hug and whispered in her ear, "You good as long as you're on your best behavior at all times."

"Okay." She placed her arms around my neck and I kissed her jaw.

"I'll get up with you another time though. I need to holla at Bizo." I let her go.

"Am I coming over tonight?"

"Nah, I got business to handle tonight."

Her eyes dropped letting me know she wasn't happy, but I couldn't worry about that right now. I kissed her jaw once more before walking away. I saw Bizo go outside, so that's where I headed. I glanced around seeing him speaking to a group of bitches. I made my way to him and when he noticed, he said something to them then met me halfway.

"Come over here and let me speak to you about some shit."

He nodded his head asking, "Everything straight?"

I didn't answer him until we were away from everyone. We stood by my car and I said, "The dancer."

He grinned asking, "Which one?"

"The main one. Jenday."

"Ooo, you feeling her fine ass hun?"

"She is sexy. I saw her a few days ago. When I saw her tonight, I believe it's fate."

"Well good luck with that shit." He chuckled.

I glanced around the parking lot. I was looking to see if she really left. I wanted to get another look at her thick ass.

"What you mean by that? That's you or something?" I didn't give a fuck, I was just being polite.

"Nah, but she's focused man. It's just her and her sister. Some shit happened with her folks. Besides these gigs, and dancing at the club, she's only focused on raising her little sister. I've known her for years, and never even heard her mentioning a man."

I nodded my head. That's a good thing. It meant she didn't have a man. That was better for me.

"She dances? Like a stripper?" I inquired.

"Nah, not really. She works at that exclusive ass gentleman's club downtown. The one you have to have a membership for. Those aren't your regular strippers. Those ladies give a whole experience. It's like burlesque. Shit is sexy as fuck. She is their best dancer. The club is packed every time she's on the schedule. She only works there three times a week. Probably make enough money to last for months at a time."

I was taking it all in. I made a mental note to find out exactly where this club was. She had me intrigued, and I had to act on it.

"I appreciate the info man, I'm about to head inside and help Orion get shit together for tonight, we open in an hour."

"Ahhight then." We slapped hands before he walked away, and I headed inside to google this club.

I spoke to people along the way as I made my way upstairs to my office. I sat behind the desk turning the computer on. I pulled up google and typed in, exclusive gentleman's club downtown Charlotte. Only one popped up, and it had to be the one. *Exquisite Gentleman's Club,* was the name. I clicked through pictures before going to the membership page. I didn't blink an eye when I filled out the form, and paid my five-hundred dollars. This better be a bomb ass club charging this much monthly.

"What you doing bruh?"

I didn't even hear him come in. Orion was standing over me with a frown.

"A gentleman's club? You gotta pay for pussy now?" He asked me.

I chuckled as I replied, "It ain't like that, man."

"Seems that way. You just paid for a five-hundred-dollar membership."

"Why you standing over my damn shoulders anyway?"

"Shit, I called your name twice."

I didn't hear that nigga at all. I raked my hand down my face and asked, "Were you here during the shoot?"

"I got here at the end." Orion replied.

"Did you see the dancer with them pretty ass loc's?"

He nodded his head and I continued to say, "This is my second time seeing her ass. It's fate."

His boisterous laugh filled the room as he exclaimed, "What, nigga?"

"Bizo told me she is a dancer at this club."

"You tryna wife a stripper?" He frowned.

I shook my head saying, "Bizo told me that its not like that there. They aren't your regular strippers and shit. More like Burlesque. They give a show."

His eyes narrowed as he glanced back at the screen.

"Put me down then. I want to see this shit."

I shook my head as I filled out another form for Orion. I guess we'll be hitting the club together.

"Ahhight, let's make sure shit straight for tonight," I said as I stood and we made our way next door.

******

The next day

I pulled up to the chop shop that the, Tre Five Mafia owned. They were a part of the crime syndicate that we stole cars for. Bizo, and Orion pulled up right after me.

We already knew to leave our guns in the car since we would get pat down at the door. Once the big ass nigga at the door confirmed we didn't have anything on us, we were led to the back office where, Puma, the leader of Tre Five was.

"What's good?" We all slapped hands with him before he offered us a seat.

"Ain't nothin'. We came to holla at you about something," I said.

"This doesn't sound too good. What's going on?" Puma asked.

"Three months and were done." Bizo, Orion, and I discussed this a few nights ago. Yes, we made good money, but at what cost? We've been shot at, and ran down on a few times. We didn't think this shit was worth our life, especially when we had income coming in from two other businesses; the club, and our gambling spot. We weren't hurtin' for shit, and we had money stacked for any rainy days.

"Damn, y'all are my best guys. I understand though, this life isn't for everyone. You all put in enough work that I don't have a problem with it."

We thought he would give us a tough time, but I was glad he didn't. Whether he liked it or not, we were done in three months.

"Shit, that was easy," said Bizo.

"Nah, I ain't trippin'. I'm not in the business of forcing people to do some shit they don't want to do," Puma replied taking a breath then pulling a piece of paper out of his desk drawer. He slid it across the table, and Orion picked it up. I leaned over taking a look to see a list of six cars.

"If you finish that list before then, you can retire early. Two million for all six." He sat back in his chair gaging out reactions.

"Shiiit, that's over a half million a piece, we can get with that," I stated. Bizo and Orion agreed. We then stood, said our goodbye's, and left.

"Yo, this shit is sweet," said Bizo.

"Hell yea, we still getting that panorama this weekend?"

"Yup. Saturday. They usually go to bed around eleven," Bizo answered.

"Cool. I'll holla at y'all." We dapped it up, got in our cars, and pulled off.

******

Bizo, Orion, and I crept up the deserted street. These people had some big ass yards over here. There were six houses spread out on the dead-end street. We traveled to the end, turned around and came back up. We parked at the house after the one we were searching for.

"Damn, this shit is going to be too easy, he parked his shit in the driveway." Orion took notice.

"Yea, that's because he didn't think niggas had the gall to take his shit." Bizo chuckled along with the rest of us.

"Ahhight, Keifon, stay in the car. We got this," Orion told me.

"Aww man, I thought I was going to have some fun tonight," I replied.

"You are…as the getaway driver. As soon as you see us pull out, you pull out too."

"I got you," I responded.

Bizo and Orion pulled their ski-mask over their faces before Bizo grabbed his tools. They crept up his driveway staring up at the bedroom window making sure we didn't see any movement.

Bizo got to work right away popping the locks. The loud glaring of the alarm went off.

"Shit," I heard exclaimed. I glanced up at the window seeing the bedroom light pop on.

"Hurry up, nigga. He up," I yelled out the car window as if the guy didn't already know we were there.

"I almost got it." Bizo was working on getting the car started. Right when he did, the front door opened.

"What the fuck y'all niggers doing?" The white guy shouted. Anger rose up my body hearing him call us that. I wanted to beat his ass, but knew time was of the essence.

Bizo hoped in the car while saying, "Come on, bruh."

I saw Orion reach to open the door, but before he could sink down in the seat, we heard loud pops. My heart dropped seeing Orion fall against the side of the car. He was hit.

"Shit, shit," I expressed as I hit the gas backing up.

"Leave, and I won't kill you," the guy screamed.

By this time; I was behind the guys car. I worked fast picking Orion up, placing him in the car and speeding off. Bizo was right behind us.

"Hang on, bro. I'm going to get you to the hospital."

He didn't say anything because I'm sure his shit was on fire. My phone rang and I answered.

"Aye, I'm going to drop the car off and get one of them niggas to bring me to the hospital. Fuck," Bizo screamed.

"See you there. I have to concentrate getting him there. Stay up, bro. Shit." I pressed the gas harder. I couldn't let shit happen to my brother man. Shit wasn't supposed to happen like this.

Oba

"Heelllp!" I heard a deep baritone resonate through the emergency department."

I glanced up seeing a tall guy holding on to another tall, but muscular guy. His shirt was covered in blood and he looked weak. I rushed over with a few other nurses and a gurney.

"Place him down gently," I told the guy. He did as I asked and we whisked the patient away.

"Y'all have to save my brother!" The guy shouted.

"We got it from here, sir. If you could, please wait in the waiting room." I pointed behind him. He glared at me for a second. It looked like he wanted to curse my ass out, understandably so.

I stepped in front of him placing my hand on his shoulder and said, "I got him. Don't worry." I smiled. He nodded his head, turned on his heels and headed to the waiting room. I saw him pull out his phone, probably calling family.

I made my way back over to his brother who was on the verge of passing out.

"Sir, what's your name?"

"O...Orion."

"Okay Orion, we are going to get you to the OR. There are no exit wounds, so the bullet, or bullets are still in there. We got you." I gave him a warm smile as we headed to the operating room.

"Quickly Page Dr. Blout," I shouted.

"He's crashing!" I shouted. I looked to his brother who stood at my words.

"Clear!" Brittany, another nurse yelled as she used the paddles against his chest. The heart monitor took a few seconds, but it began to beep again. I gave his brother a reassuring smile as we rushed to the OR.

An hour later, Dr. Blout had removed the bullet, repaired the tissue, and stitched him up. We were now in the recovery room. He had to stay in here until we found him a bed upstairs. He was still down from the anesthesia, but should be waking up any minute now.

I got word that an officer was in the ER waiting to speak to him. We were required to call them when a gunshot victim comes in. After I checked his vitals, I went out front to speak to the Officer.

"Good evening, sir. You're here for our GSV?"

"Yes, ma'am. Do you know what happened?"

"No I don't. But that's his brother who brought him in right there." I pointed to the waiting room to his brother who now had an older gentleman sitting beside him. They both looked distraught waiting on word from their family member. I was glad that tonight we had good news to share.

Dr. Blout walked up beside me shaking hands with the Officer.

"Let us give an update first, then you can have a word with him."

"No problem," the Officer replied.

I fell in step with Dr. Blout as he approached the two men.

"Family of Orion Russell?" He confirmed.

"Yes, Doctor. I am his father, Jahamal, and this is my other son, Keifon." Whom I now knew was their father shook Dr. Blout's hand.

"How is my boy?" He questioned with a strained look on his face.

"He was shot once in the chest…."

"How is he?" Another guy rushed in.

"The Doc telling us now. I'm sorry Dr. Blout, go ahead," Jahamal stated.

"He was shot once in the chest just an inch away from his heart. We were able to remove the bullet with no issues. He was lucky. He is in recovery now, but will be moved to a room as soon as one becomes available." Dr. Blout informed them.

All three of them let out a sigh of relief. The father thanked Dr. Blout.

The Doctor then turned his head to the Officer motioning for him to come over. "This is Officer, Wilson. He has a few questions for you. Oba here will come get you once Mr. Russell is situated in a room." Dr. Blout and I then walked away leaving the men with the Officer.

I wanted to keep an eye on Orion, therefore I made my way back to recovery. I noticed that his eyes were slowly opening. He winched in pain when he tried to move.

"Don't move, Mr. Russell. Just rest. You were shot once. Dr. Blout removed the bullet. You are going to be fine." I gave a subtle smile.

Orion was a handsome man. Fine as hell if I'm really being honest. I watched as his eyes fluttered shut as I admired him from head to toe. His skin was smooth the color of Almonds with tattoos decorating his chest, and right arm. He was solid with muscles for days. He had a low cut with perfect waves. His eyes fluttered back open as he whispered, "Can you stare any harder. I know a nigga fine and shit, but damn." The right side of his mouth lifted weakly into a smile.

I rolled my eyes saying, "Please, I'm just making sure you're still breathing."

He gazed at me with a 'yea right', look on his face causing me to chortle.

"Oba, we have a bed for him on the sixth floor. Room 2612. We are about to move him if you want to go ahead and gather his family," Brittany announced.

"Okay Brit," I replied before walking away.

"Hey, if you want to follow me, they are moving him to a room now." I said once I got to the waiting room.

His family stood up and we headed to the elevators. Everyone was silent as we road the elevators up and stepped off headed to the room. When we stepped in, Brittany was settling him in. Once he was situated, she left out leaving me alone with the four men. For some reason, I didn't want to leave his side.

"Oba, can I please get some of that good ass ice and water?" Orion asked.

"Sure, but I should warn you, it's going to hurt like hell when it goes down."

"I can handle it," he replied. I nodded my head in understanding before walking out.

"Girl, that man is fine," said Brittany as we stood there while I filled the pitcher with ice and water.

"He's alright." I giggled.

"Girl, is something wrong with your eyes? That man is fine as fuck, and he has a thing for you."

I stopped what I was doing and turned towards her and frowned, "He doesn't even know me?"

"He doesn't have to. He sees that you're beautiful and that ass poking out." We both chuckled. She was right, I noticed him admiring me.

"It's unethical," was my reply.

"He wont be a patient forever. Just the next two to three days."

"Uhh, you get on my nerves." I turned and walked away as she giggled.

When I walked back into the room, the guys ceased all conversation. I knew they were probably talking about what really happened, because I know they didn't tell the police the real story. They were probably up to no good, but that wasn't my business.

I filled a paper cup with water and held it out for him.

"Uhn, Oba, can you help me out. I can't reach it."

I rolled my eyes knowing his ass was playing. I shook my head as I opened a straw sticking it inside the cup and holding it to his lips.

"You doing too much," I expressed.

"How?" He asked before taking a sip.

"You not slick, Mr. Russell."

"Orion," he replied.

"What?"

"My name is Orion?"

I didn't say anything else. I placed the cup down and told him, "Press this button if you need someone." I pointed to the button that was attached to a cord.

"I'll press the button if I need you," he stated and his family chuckled.

"You wild man," I heard one of them say as I left out of the room. Mr. Orion is something else. Brittany noticed the smile on my face and asked, "Was I right?"

I rolled my eyes and stated, "Possibly," before walking back down to the ER.

Orion

"How the fuck you tryna spit game and you've been shot the fuck up?" Keifon questioned me.

"That's going to be wifey right there," I replied.

I glanced over at my Pops. He was sitting in a chair with his elbows on his knees. His eyes moved to me as he asked, "What the fuck happened?"

"The alarm on the car went off and the man came outside blasting," Bizo replied to him.

"Y'all need to stop this shit right now." Jahamal demanded.

"We gave Puma our notice. We have five more cars to get. We already agreed," said Keifon.

"I don't care what the fuck y'all agreed too." My Pops stood up towering over my bed before continuing to say, "Fuck them five cars. You almost lost your life, son."

I huffed as I struggled to sit up. My Pops helped me out. Once settled sitting up a little, I said, "Pops, you know we can't do that. If we do, we as good as dead anyway."

He raked his hand down his face and replied, "Let me talk to him. I can't have this. Your mother will have my head knowing that I knew about this."

"Nah, Mr. Jahamal, you know it doesn't work that way. We gave our word," Bizo replied.

My Pops shook his head. He knew Bizo was right, therefore he didn't continue with that conversation. Instead he asked, "How you feeling, son?"

"My chest hurts like hell, but other than that, I'm alive."

"Bizo, you dropped that off?"

"Oh, y'all still got the car?" Pops asked.

"Hell yea, we did. I dropped it off and told Puma what was up. He sent his prayers and said if we need anything, to let him know."

"Cool," I replied. They stayed with me for a few more hours before leaving. It didn't take long for me to fall asleep, I was tired as hell.

I woke up some hours later to a beautiful sight. Oba was standing over me with a clipboard in her handwriting something down.

"What you writing?"

"Your vitals," she replied.

"They good?"

"Yes."

"You are beautiful, you know that?"

"I've been told a time or two," she replied causing me to chuckle. Yea, she knew she was fine as wine.

"You going to let a nigga take you out and shit when I get out of here?"

She placed the clipboard down and then her eyes fell on mine. She smiled and I saw it before she said anything. She was about to turn my ass down.

"You know I can't do that. You're my patient."

"Yea, but I won't be in a few days."

She sighed then said, "Orion, I'm sorry, but I cannot."

"You can. You just don't want to. A nigga been shot, and you can't even comfort me?" I gave her the puppy dog face and she fell out laughing.

"I'm sure you are a nice man, but this can't happen."

"That's fucked up, Oba. What kind of name is that anyway, where you from?"

"Nigeria, but I have been here since middle school."

"Ooo, I got me an African Goddess."

She reached in her scrubs for the third time. Her pretty ass frowned before sliding it back in her pocket. I don't know who the hell that was. I hope it wasn't her man because he was going to have to move over. A real nigga stepping in.

She lifted her arm checking the time on her watch. She glanced at me and said, "It's almost time for me to get off. You'll have another nurse. I guess I'll see you on my next shift."

"I hope so, baby. I'm willing to ask to stay for an extra day just so I can see you."

"You have issues. It doesn't work like that."

"Ohhh, Ahhhh." I squeezed my eyes tightly, and she stepped closer to me and asked, "What's wrong?"

I held on to my chest until she was right in my face. I then smiled gazing up at her and replied, "See, I can get an extra day if I have too."

"Don't do that shit no more, that's not funny. Don't you know that you are hurt for real?"

"I'm just fuckin' wit' you. Calm down," I chuckled.

"I don't play like that. I'll see you later." She stomped out of the room. I couldn't do nothing but shake my head. Her little Nigerian ass is going to be a handful. I became drowsy again. I closed my eyes, and took my ass back to damn sleep.

Chapter 3

Keifon

I pulled up to my parents house to pick up my mom. She was upset last night that my Pops didn't allow her to come to the hospital. It was late, and he told her to go back to sleep and he would keep her updated. She fought him about it, but eventually gave in.

My Pops was currently at work. He had an event that he and a couple of his employees had to do security for. It was some type of convention for city officials. Yes, my Pops doing the damn thang. He has the best security firm in Charlotte.

I stepped out of my car looking up and down the street. The little boy that lived next door was riding his bike with his sister.

"Hey Keifon," he shouted when he noticed me and rode his bike faster to get to me.

"What's up, man?"

"Can I get five dollars?"

I chuckled glancing towards his house. His mother stepped on the porch with some little ass shorts showing her thick thighs and a tiny t-shirt with her breast on full display.

"TJ, are you bothering Keifon again? Hey Keifon."

"Heey Ms. Parker." I joked referencing the movie, Friday. She giggled moving her attention back to her son.

"Come on, TJ, I'm sure he has things to do."

"He straight, Sandy."

"What you want money for lil' man?"

"I want my momma to take me to the store, but she said she don't have no money." He pouted. TJ was eight years old and he was always respectful towards me. I didn't mind giving him a few dollars. I dug in my pocket and peeled off a twenty.

"Boy, you begging for money?" Sandy asked with her hand on her hip drawing my attention to her body.

"Ma, I'm just getting money for the store, dang."

"Whoa, buddy. Don't talk to your mother like that." I yanked the twenty-dollar bill back.

He looked towards the ground saying, "Sorry."

"Don't tell me, tell your momma."

He glanced over at his momma and said, "I'm sorry momma." He turned back towards me asking, "Can I have that money now?"

"As long as you promise never to talk to your momma like that again."

"I promise," he replied.

I pulled another twenty off handing him both of them and said, "Make sure you get your sister something too."

"I will, thank you Keifon." He then peddled his little legs riding his bike back into his driveway where his sister and momma was. I saw him show his momma the money and she thanked me.

I took a step towards the house, but my momma, Iris, was already coming out the door. I rounded the car opening the door for her.

"What's up, pretty lady?" I hugged her, and kissed her jaw.

"Hey baby, you out here flirting with Sandy again?"

She sank down in the seat as I replied, "Nah, I was breaking her son off with a few bills."

"Oh okay, come on so you can take me to see my other big baby."

I chuckled as I shut her door and rounded the back of the car getting in on the drivers side. I crank up the car, then backed out of the driveway before pulling forward heading towards Novant Health.

Within twenty minutes, I was parking my car in the parking deck. I got out and then let my mother out. She looped her arm around mine as I hit the alarm and we made our way inside. We stopped to the front desk giving our names then we were given visitor passes to stick on our shirts. We then made our way to the elevators. I pressed the number for his floor and the elevator slowly moved upwards.

We trailed the hallways until we got to Orion's room. My mother went in first and when Orion saw her, he smiled. I could tell he was still a little weak, but at least he was able to sit up without noticeable pain.

"Hey baby." Our mothers voice trembled upon seeing her son in the state that he was in. I walked over to the bed giving my brother dap, before I sat in the chair against the window and let my mother have her time.

"Hey Ma. Give your favorite son a hug." He stretched his right arm out and she gently fell into the hug.

"Stop boy, you know I don't play favorites." She chuckled before continuing to say, "I was so worried about you last night." Tears were welling in her eyes. I hate that we had to lie to her, but it was for the best.

I stood to my feet taking the two steps to Orion's bed and comforted her. I reached over rubbing her back saying, "It's okay Ma, he is okay. His stubborn ass wouldn't leave us." I chuckled trying to make light of the situation. It worked because my mother smiled as she wiped the tears that had fallen from her eyes.

"Yea Ma, I'm good. Ya boy gonna always be good."

She looked at him sideways while asking, "Now tell me what happened."

Orion and I shared a look as to say, *lie nigga*. Before one of us opened our mouth she said, "And don't lie to me."

I sighed and stated, "We don't know Ma. We were leaving the club and shots rang out when we pulled out the parking lot."

Iris wasn't dumb, our mother was a smart woman. She sensed we were lying, and we knew it when her lips poked out and she gave us the side eye.

"That's the same thing your daddy said. Sounds rehearsed to me."

"Don't trip Momma, ain't no body lying to you." I was indeed lying through my teeth but for good reason. We didn't want her to worry.

"Okay." Her voice was small. When she got like that she was thinking. She sat in the chair beside the bed but kept her eyes on me.

There was a knock on the door, and a nurse stepped in.

"Hey, Mr. Russell." She smiled brightly.

Orion started shaking his head. My mother and I frowned wondering what that was about.

"I don't want you, where is Oba?"

"Orion," my mother exclaimed.

"I'm sorry Ma, I just want to see my future wife."

This dude was crazy. The nurse wasn't even fazed. She walked over to the bed and began checking his vitals.

"Oba will be in in a few. You want me to send her in here when she gets here?"

"Please."

She giggled while saying, "I'm Brittany, and I told Oba that you were feeling her. This proves my point."

"What she say when you said that?" Orion inquired.

"She acted like she wasn't worried about you, but that smile said differently."

"Oh word?"

"Yes, but in the meantime, I'm going to continue to check you out."

Orion didn't say anything else. He had a goofy grin on his face. I guess he was thinking about Oba's ass. The nurse, Brittany left out of the room giving us our privacy back.

"Orion, you can't talk to people like that," my mother stated.

"What?" He acted innocent. He knew exactly what he did, and momma don't play that shit. She doesn't care how old we are, she will smack us upside our head just like she just did.

"Maaaan, why you have to hit me, Ma?"

"Because you being disrespectful."

"I'm sorry Ma, I wasn't trying to be disrespectful, I just want to see my baby."

"Boy, I can't wait until this girl comes to work. I have to see her." We all chuckled.

My momma went down to the cafeteria to get us something to eat. We were in the middle of our meal when we heard a knock on the door.

"Come on in," said my momma.

The door pushed open and Oba walked in. My brother was all smiles at this point. I don't know what's going on in his mind, but Oba must really have that niggas attention. He ain't never acted like this over a damn woman.

Oba smiled as she said, "Hey, I hear you've been causing trouble in here today." She placed her hand on her hip.

"Nah, a nigga just wanted to see your sexy ass."

Our mother stood up and reached her hand out to Oba saying, "Hey, I'm Iris, their mother." Oba shook her hand while saying,

"Hi, Mrs. Iris. Your son has been giving me trouble while he's been here," Oba snitched.

"Oh really?" Our mother raised her eyebrow turning towards Orion as she continued to say, "Now Orion, you know I didn't raise you like that."

"Maaaan…" Orion started but was cut off by our mother again when she said, "Apologize Orion."

Orion huffed, and Oba had a smirk on her face. Orion kissed his teeth before saying, "My bad Oba. I apologize. Damn, I can't believe you are doing me like this. How we getting married and shit and you snitching to my momma."

Oba's reply was a cute giggle as she walked over to my brothers bed holding up a tiny white cup with a pill in it as she shrugged.

"It's the truth Orion. Here is your dose of hydrocodone." She handed him the pill, then filled his cup with water handing that to him as well.

"I see how it is baby," he replied before taking the pill then sitting the cups on the small table that was over his lap.

Oba chortled as she checked his wound and changed his bandages. Orion's eyes stayed on her.

"Bro, you got it bad." I laughed along with my mother.

"Ms. Oba, I think you're in trouble."

"Why you say that, Mrs. Iris?"

"My son seems to be feeling you something terrible. Women fall at his feet, and you are not. Get ready girl, he about to be on you like white on rice.."

"Maaaaa, stop." Orion shook his head while smiling.

"What baby, it's the truth. And you are right. She is beautiful."

I watched Oba blush. She was trying not to smile, but I saw it. She was feeling my brother and I have a feeling that he is not going to be able to resist her.

"Well after he is released, he probably won't see me anymore."

Orion scoffed, "We'll see about that."

Oba gave him the side eye before announcing that she'd be back later and left the room.

"I like her," our mother stated.

"I do too, Ma."

"You know, she isn't the type that will take your mess. I know how you are. If you are truly not ready to be faithful, leave her alone."

"Noted, Ma," Orion replied as sleep began taking over his body from that pain peel.

******

Nighttime came quick after being at the hospital with Orion with my mother. After I dropped her off at the house, I came home and did a little research.

Jenday was on my mind something serious. I sat in my den that I made into an office behind my desk. I pulled up, *Exquisite's,* website to see the line-up for the night. It only gave stage names. I saw, Passion, Lovely Queen, and Diamond.

"Shit," I expressed not getting the information I needed. Even with that said, I decided to shower and get dressed and head to the club hoping that Jenday was there.

I pulled up to the club at ten o'clock. I didn't want to take the chance of missing her. I gave my name at the door and was pat down and then let in. Music filled the building and a lady was on stage. The way her body was moving, was sexy. She wasn't who I was looking for though. I made my way to the bar and ordered a beer. Once it was in my hand, I found a vacant table near the front and took a seat. The club was almost to capacity. I don't know if it was truly for Jenday, but it seemed like Bizo was right.

The men and women in here looked like they were loaded with money. I was glad I decided to dress in a tailored suit or I wouldn't have been let in. The club was definitely upscale decorated in gold, white, and red. Tables were scattered throughout the main floor. There was an upstairs area where people were leaning over the banister getting a look at the woman on the stage.

Five minutes later, claps filled the room when Diamonds set was over. Another woman was introduced, but it still wasn't Jenday. I was chillin' sippin' my drink until that woman left the stage.

"The time has come for your favorite lady of the hour…" I tuned the DJ out having a feeling this was it. The way everyone was whistling and cheering, it had to be her. The lights dimmed as the DJ shouted, "Let's give it up for, Lovely Queen."

I watched as the red curtain slowly opened. All you could see was her silhouette, but I knew it was her. I sat up straight in my seat focused on all the curves in front of my. Got damn, her body was sick.

The sultry music played in the background as she began to wind her body. She turned facing the crowd with her sexy ass. She had the attention of every single person in the club, women included.

Jenday had on a two-piece outfit made like the one she wore for the video shoot, but it was yellow instead of black. I licked my lips as she dropped down to the ground with her ass in the air facing the crowd. She slowly stood up and gripped the pole. She climbed all the way to the top the hung upside down with her strong thighs holding her up.

"Shit." Came out in a whisper. She lifted herself back up and spun around the pole. When she got to the bottom, she landed in a split. This woman was the truth. She had my damn dick hard. I had to place my hands in my lap to try and cover it.

Jenday stood up and her eyes caught mine. She winked her eye and continued with her dance. At that moment, everyone else disappeared. It was like she was focused on me. I don't know if she really was, but it definitely felt like it. Her eyes held me captive as she danced sexily for the rest of her set. I smiled at her and she smiled back. I know it was probably a part of her act, but I didn't care. Money was being thrown and when I realized it, I stood making my way the few steps to the stage while digging in my pocket. I had at least a band on this roll. I made it rain on that stage. She dropped back to her knees and crawled sexily towards me. People were cheering her on as she stopped in front of me, got on her back and spread her legs quickly making the tip of her shoes hit the floor by her head.

"Damn." I stood wide eyed. She was the truth. She was now back on her knees grabbing my head placing it between her sweet-smelling breast. I was in awe. She leaned down and whispered in my ear, "stalker." I could do nothing but laugh. She kissed my jaw then moved away finishing her set the same way it started. With the lights dim and only her silhouette showing. The curtain then closed and the lights came back on. Someone came out to collect her money in a plastic bag.

I was done here, I wasn't going to wait around for her. I would find her another time. I don't think she's ready to admit that she's my future yet. I grabbed my beer, downing the rest, before leaving the club with a hard dick. I dialed Prissy's number instructing her to meet me at the house. She was asleep, but of course she agreed.

Jenday

I made my way off stage heading towards the back. I was getting dressed when James entered my room with my bag of money.

"Thank you, James."

"No problem baby. Aye, you knew ol' boy you were all over?"

"I've seen him a time or two, but I don't know him. Why?"

"No reason, just asking." He then left out of the room. James had been trying to holla at me since I started working here two years ago. I'm not attracted to him though. He's a nice man, but he isn't a looker. I know it's not all about looks, but I at least have to be able to look at you and be turned on. Plus, I love a tall man. He is only five feet nine.

For some reason, Keifon being their watching me made me go harder. He was just so damn handsome. He was dressed exquisitely in a navy-blue tailored suit. Far different from how I've seen him dressed before.

I hurriedly grabbed my things and headed out front in search of his stalking ass. I know Bizo was the one that told him I worked here. He saw me in my element and I can tell he was mesmerized. I walked past people showing their love of my set. I know I'm bad. I told everyone thanks as I roamed around the club with my bag on my shoulder. I was searching for Keifon, but didn't see him anywhere.

I asked one of the ladies at the bar, "Did you see the guy who approached the stage when I was doing my set?"

"Yea girl, he left right after your walked off the stage."

"Thank you, Trina." I walked off. For some reason, I was upset that he came up here to see me and left like that. I trekked to my Nissan Altima and got in heading home. I usually stop and get me some chicken nuggets from Wendy's or Cookout to appease my appetite, but Leah texted me letting me know that she cooked dinner and saved me a plate. She seemed happier; I didn't know what that was about but I love seeing my sister happy. She has been through so much at an early age; we both have. I know how to keep myself together though. I've only broke down in front of her twice that I can remember; when our mother died, and when I realized I wasn't going to be able to start living my dream by going to Julliard.

I parked in the driveway, grabbed my bag, and got out the car. When I opened the door, Leah's head popped up from the couch. She normally waited up for me when I work at the club. She says she has to make sure I'm safe before she can really fall asleep because I'm really all she has considering our father ain't shit. I pray everyday that he can get himself together. At least for my sister. She has needed him this whole time, and he just doesn't care. I will never understand how after my mother died, he didn't go to rehab to let me live my life, and take care of Leah. Honestly, I still wouldn't trust him to do right by her. Even if he would have gotten clean, I probably still would have chosen not to go, or I would have took her with me. It would have been hard training, and working to pay bills and take care of her, but it would have been worth it. I love my sister that much.

"Hey, kid." I walked over to her placing a kiss to her temple. She shushed me as she smiled and replied, "Hey sis, Daddy is in his room asleep."

I understood now, she was happy that our Dad was home. I made my way to his bedroom peeking inside. Our father was knocked out. I silently closed the door letting him get his rest, then went to take a shower. I would speak to him in the morning. When I walked in the kitchen, Leah was no longer in the living room, but my sizzling hot plate was on the kitchen table. I sat down and scarfed down my barbecued chicken, green beans, and rice. Leah could cook her ass off. I was grateful for that. She helped me out a lot even though I told her just to focus on school and I would handle the rest.

When I finished eating, I cleaned up my mess and headed to my bedroom. As soon as my head hit the pillow, I was out.

I woke up the next morning to laughter and the smell of good food. I lay there for a minute with a smile on my face listening to the two. My father sounded so happy. My smile faded once the thought of him leaving again for God knows how long.

I got up swinging my legs over the side of the bed stretching my arms high in the air. Shit, that stretch felt good. I stood and headed into the bathroom to relieve my bladder and take care of my morning hygiene. I then made my way barefoot through the house until Leah and my father came into view.

"Good morning, sweetheart." Keith was the first to see me and speak.

"Good morning, Daddy." I leaned down kissing his jaw and hugging him tightly. I held on a little longer, getting all the love I could get since I didn't know when it would be snatched away.

"Good morning, sis. Your plate is in the microwave and your fruit is in the refrigerator."

"Thank you, sis." I said before making my way to the microwave and cutting it on while I grabbed my bowl of fruit out of the refrigerator. I then pulled my plate out when the microwave beeped and sat down in front of my Dad.

"This French toast looks good, sis."

"Thank you," she replied with a smile.

I took my first bite before asking my Dad, "How long will you be here this time?"

"Jenday," Leah shouted. My eyes moved to her. I tilted my head to the side wondering why she was yelling. Well I knew why, but she also knew why I asked.

"It's okay, Leah. I don't have the best history when it comes to you girls, and I apologize for that. I don't know when things got so bad, then losing your mother made it worse."

I wasn't hearing none of that. It wasn't an excuse to me. He should want to do better for us. My father actually looked good. He didn't look like a crackhead when he cleaned himself up. He was a functioning crackhead. I honestly believe he could stop if he wanted too, and it was obvious that he didn't.

"Jenday, I am proud of you for stepping in when I couldn't."

"How long?" I asked again.

"It ain't no telling." He sighed raking his hand down his scruffy face.

I took another bite of my food before saying, "Well at least let me shape your hair, and clean your facial hair."

"Okay, sweetheart." The rest of our breakfast was eaten in silence. I noticed the gloomy look on Leah's face. She would be alright though. I will make sure of it. I am always left to pick up the pieces every time he left.

I cleaned the kitchen since Leah cooked, then got my clippers and headed to the bathroom with my father behind me. He sat in the chair that he pulled inside and let me clean him up.

I learned to cut hair when he refused to go to the barbershop years ago. I think he was embarrassed about how he is and didn't want people questioning him. Which I didn't understand because like I mentioned, he doesn't look bad.

"Jenday, you know I love you girls, right?"

"Yes Daddy, I know. Just not enough to get clean," I replied.

He didn't say anything else, and I didn't either. It took me about thirty minutes to get him right. He offered to sweep the hair up and I let him while I went to search for Leah. She was on her bed laying on her stomach crying.

"Hey, hey, what's wrong?"

She turned around so that I could see her and said, "I know he's just going to leave. I'm sorry for yelling at you, I just wish he would get himself together. We already lost mommy."

I sat beside her, pulling her up and engulfed her in my arms. I consoled her letting her know that I would always be there. I glanced up at the door seeing my father stand there with tears in his eyes. I held eye contact with him until he turned and walked away. I could only shake my head.

Eventually Leah calmed down and fell asleep. I tucked her in and left out of her room in search of my father. We needed to talk and I wasn't going to hold shit back. He needed to be a responsible fucking adult. I'm sick of his shit.

I found him sitting on the back porch smoking a Newport. He turned his body hearing the door creak open. He took one look at the scowl on my face and turned around saying, "I don't want to hear it, sweetheart. I know I'm a fuck up."

I made sure the door was closed before taking a seat beside him. I stared out into our huge backyard before focusing my attention on him.

"Daddy, I love you, but you know you are wrong. Forget how I feel, Leah is devastated every time you up and leave. She cries for you and guess who has to be there to console her? Me! I have no problem with that, but I know it would be beneficial for you to come around more. Shit, you need to get yourself clean and stay."

I waited at least three minutes while he puffed on that cigarette not saying anything. When he finally spoke I was furious. In a low voice he stated, "I'm not ready." I shook my head as I got up leaving him by himself. There was no use.

Oba

I made my way to the elevator heading upstairs to care for a few patients. They had me traveling from the emergency department to upstairs today. I didn't mind though, sometimes I needed a break from the hustle and bustle of the ER.

I felt my phone vibrate in the pocket of my scrubs. Since I was in the elevator, I reached for it and rolled my eyes seeing that it was Tommy once again. I silenced my phone and placed it right back in my pocket. I don't know if he thought I was playing with his ass or what, but I don't play that putting your hands on a woman shit. He doesn't stand a chance with me. He should have just dealt with the fact that I wasn't looking for a man.

I stepped off the elevator and checked in at the nurses station on the sixth floor.

"Whew chile, it is busy down there," I said to Brittany who was standing there reading over a chart.

"I know you are glad to be up here for a little while."

"Yes I am." I reached for a chart looking it over.

"Girl, you may as well put that down and head to your man. He has been complaining again that we were checking on him instead of you."

I smiled shaking my head. Orion is something else. Seems like his mother was right, he doesn't give up so easily.

"I see you smiling. You may as well give that man your number. He gets out of here today. I know if it were me, I would have been given him my number. Trust me, I tried.

My smile faded. I don't know why, but her saying she tried to holla pissed me off. I mean, he wasn't even my man. Brittany burst out laughing before saying, "See, I knew your ass was going to feel some type of way. I'm just playing with you." I chuckled telling her, "You so crazy. He is going to have to wait until I see Mr. Ragland, and Mrs. Terry." I grabbed those charts and stepped away to check on those two patients. Once I was sure they were straight, I returned their charts and grabbed Orion's.

I gently knocked on his door listening for permission to step in. Once I was granted entry, I stepped in and his eyes lit up.

"There goes my baaaabbyyy," he sang imitating Usher. He had a nice ass voice too. Shit. I had to squeeze my thighs together.

"You silly."

"I've been looking for you all day, baby. My day is better now that you're here."

I rolled my eyes listening to him spit game. It was cute though. If I were being real, I wouldn't mind giving him my number and getting to know him a little better. He seems cool, and down to earth. A significant difference from Tommy's up tight ass.

I checked his vitals and changed his bandage. My phone went off for the third time. I pulled it out my pocket after I removed my plastic gloves. I grunted as I sent Tommy to voicemail once again.

"Damn, I wish this dude get the point." I groaned. I didn't even mean to say it out loud.

I glanced at Orion and he had a frown on his face as he asked, "What's up with that? That's your man?"

I was shaking my head before he even finished asking his question. "Not at all. We were talking but I had to let him go."

Orion nodded his head as he replied, "He has to be a fucking fool to let your fine African Queen ass go."

"He didn't really have a choice in the matter. He did some foul shit and I had to send him on his way."

"That's better for me, what he do though? I want to make sure I don't make that same mistake."

I smirked not knowing why I was contemplating telling this stranger my business, but for some reason, he seemed easy to talk to. I was actually enjoying his company.

"Unless you are a woman beater, I doubt it."

Orion sat up abruptly and groaned. I helped him sit up and he asked, "That nigga put his hands on you?"

I nodded my head as I admitted, "He choked me. I told him I wasn't interested in being exclusive right now and he choked me."

"What's that niggas full name?"

I could tell he was mad as hell. He had this look in his eye that made me shiver. If he were down for me and we didn't even know each other, I can't imagine how he would be if we actually talked.

"Tommy Strum."

"Ahhight, I got you."

"What you going to do?"

"The less you know, the better, baby."

I didn't ask anymore questions. He asked me to get him fresh ice and I did. When I came back in the room, he had his phone sitting on the table smiling at me.

"Oh lord." I rolled my eyes.

"I'm saying, let me get that number."

I wasn't even going to try and fight it anymore. I lifted his phone entering my number. He was all smiles at this point. My phone buzzed in my pocket and again it was Tommy.

"Let me see your phone." Without asking questions I handed it to him.

"Yea." He had the phone on speaker and no one said anything.

"Yo." Orion spoke again.

"Who is this?"

"You called my girl's phone?"

"Your girl, I was just in that pussy." Tommy chuckled.

"I bet you won't get that shit again. Call her phone again and see what's going to happen."

"I will fuc…" Orion hung up.

"He's been warned. Let me know if he gives you anymore problems."

"Okay, well, I'm going to get out of here. I'll come back when the doctor is ready to discharge you."

"Okay, with your sexy ass." I smiled as I left out of the room. I went about my day until it was time for him to be released. As promised, I met him in the room. His mother was there waiting. He requested that I be the one to walk him down. I agreed since we weren't too busy on this floor. Usually we have transport do it, but my supervisor said it was okay since I was headed back to the emergency department anyway.

"You going to answer when I call right?" He asked while we were waiting out front for his mother.

"Of course," I replied.

His mother pulled in front of us and I wheeled him to the car before putting the brakes on on the wheelchair.

"Can I get a hug?"

"Orion, leave this girl alone."

"What, Ma?" He chuckled and she only shook her head. The woman knew her son.

I giggled but I still helped him stand and gave him a hug. He held on tight sniffing my neck.

"Mmm, you smell good."

"Thank you," I replied as he let me go.

"Remember what I said about dude." He stated before easing down into the car.

"I won't." I responded before closing the door and making my way back inside with my lips curved in a smile. This man was something else. I'm excited to see where this goes.

Orion

"You're staying with us for a few days, right?" My mother asked as she pulled off.

"Ma, come on now. I'm not handicapped."

"No your not, but I don't feel comfortable with you by yourself right now."

I didn't want to go to my parents house, but I also knew she wasn't going to take no for an answer.

"Okay, Ma, only for a few days."

I looked over to see a content smile on her face. My momma is my baby. The smile that was plastered on her face was contagious.

When we pulled up to the house, my Dad was standing on the porch smoking a cigar. He put it out sitting it on the table when he saw us. Making his way to the car, he opened the door for my mother, hugged her then rushed over to my side of the car. He gripped my arm saying, "How you feeling, son?"

"Much better than the first day. I'm still in a little pain, but I will be alright. I'm blessed."

"Yes you are."

"Shit, I forgot to stop by the pharmacy and pick up your medicine." My mother slapped her forehead before continuing to say, "I will be right back."

"You want me to go, babe?"

"No Jahamal, I got it. Thank you, though." She got in the car cranking it up, and waited until I stepped away to back out of the driveway.

"Your mother talked you into staying here, hun?"

I chuckled before replying, "Yea, you know I'd do anything to make her happy, though. I'm probably going to be sleep the whole time. I'm tired as fuck. You can't get any sleep in the hospital. I swear those nurses were coming in there every other hour waking me up and shit."

My Dad chuckled as we walked into the house. He asked if I needed anything right now and I let him know I needed a damn blunt. I haven't smoked since I was shot and I needed to relax.

"I got you. Lets go out back."

"Nah, I want to shower first. I will be back down in a minute."

I slowly walked up the stairs to my bedroom and straight to my bathroom that was in my room. I was moving slowly, and it hurt like hell, but I felt dirty. I stayed in the shower for fifteen minutes before getting out dressing in a pair of basketball shorts, and a t-shirt.

I then headed back downstairs to see my Dad rolling a blunt on the couch. When he saw me, he stood and followed me to the back porch. I sat in one chair and he sat in another before he lit the end of the blunt taking a few puffs before handing it to me.

I took a long pull holding in the smoke before releasing it. My eyes closed letting the smoke take over my body.

"Damn, I needed this."

"I'm glad your okay, son. I don't know what your mother, brother, and I would have done if something had happened to you. That was the scariest phone call I've ever received. I think I want to come with y'all on these last few jobs."

"Man, I can't let you do that." I shook my head before I continued to say, "We just have to be extra careful, you feel me? Plus, how the hell would we explain that to Ma if things go left."

He stared at me intently. I could tell he wanted to say something, but he reframed from doing so.

"Don't worry, Pops. We going to knock this shit out and be done."

He nodded his head and we continued smoking until the blunt was a roach and he put it out. We sat out back a little longer before heading back inside. I went straight to my bedroom and got in bed falling asleep in minutes.

******

Two days later

"Good morning, Orion." My mother spoke when I walked into the kitchen. She was cooking breakfast, while my Pops sat at the table drinking a cup of coffee.

"Good morning, Ma. How are you this morning?"

"Oh, I'm good. How's your pain level?"

"I'm at a six right now. Not too bad. I just took a pain pill, so I'll be straight for a while."

She nodded as I spoke to my Pops before sitting down. I also let them know, "I'm headed out after breakfast for a while. Keifon coming to scoop me."

"What, are you sure you're okay to be out?"

"Yea, I'm just going up to the hospital to take Oba something as a thank you. I won't be gone long."

"This girl is going to change your life." She giggled.

"Come on now. But shiiit, you might be right." All three of us chuckled.

Oba has been on my mind since I left the hospital. The way she fit into my arms when we hugged was perfect. I haven't called her yet, because I've been in and out of it for the past two days catching up on my rest.

My mother cooked chocolate chip pancakes, scrambled cheese eggs, bacon, and cheese grits. My mother knows I love me some damn pancakes. As soon as she placed my plate in front of me, I dug in. She placed a glass of apple juice in front of me before taking a seat in front of my Pops.

"So, tell me more about this young lady that has you smitten?" My mother asked before pouring syrup ok her pancakes.

I smiled as I replied, "Well, she is from Nigeria. She says she's been in the states since middle school. That's all I really know besides, she is beautiful and cool as shit. But I'm going to get to know her. Ma, you know I've never been interested in a woman like this. She is intriguing."

"Wow, Nigerian. I agree with you on the beautiful part I see why she has your head gone already."

"I don't know about all that, Ma. Only time will tell."

My father had a smirk on his face. I could see his mind moving a mile a minute.

"What's up Pops. I can see you want to say something."

He held his hands up in surrender as he said, "Aye, if you like it, I love it. I think it's good that you came across a woman that is worth your time. Only thing I have to say is, those Africans don't play. She's not going to give you chance after chance, so if she is really who you want, treat her right. You have to let those other hoes go."

My Pops was a real one. He didn't hold anything back. He always kept it one hunnid with us. He has no filter either.

"Your father is right, Orion. I hope you know what you're doing."

"I will get right for her."

We ate the rest of our food and then my mother cleaned the kitchen while my father and I stepped onto the back porch for our morning blunt.

"What's good Bro, Pops."

"Hey, son."

"What's good, bro?" I slapped hands with Keifon when he stepped onto the back porch.

"Y'all smoking without a nigga?"

"Here with your cry baby ass." I handed him the blunt as he sat down.

"I'm about to go get dressed. I'll be ready in a few." I stood up heading inside. Thirty minutes later, we were out the door.

I had Keifon take me to the flower shop, and the edible arrangements store. Once I got all I needed, Keifon drove to the hospital.

He parked the car once we arrived. I texted Oba before we left and she stated that she took a break at one. It was now 12:55. I waited until one on the dot before I called her phone.

"Hello," she sang.

"Hey, baby. I'm outside near the ER."

"What are you doing here, Orion?"

"I got something for you. Come on out."

"Give me two minutes." We then hung up the phone.

Keifon and I sat waiting for her. When she emerged from the building, I stepped out of the car.

"You should be resting Orion."

"I know, but I had to see you." I gently pulled her towards me engulfing her in a hug. She hugged me back and when I pulled away, I opened the back door pulling out the flowers, and edible arrangement handing it to her.

"I wanted to show my appreciation of you taking care of a nigga."

"Thank you, they are beautiful. But it's my job, you didn't have too." She smelled the flowers.

"No, I didn't. But I did anyway." I smiled and she smiled back.

"What time you getting off?"

"Seven."

"Alright, well I know you have to go eat and shit. Call me when you get off."

"Okay." She replied and I leaned in kissing her cheek. She then turned around walking off putting an extra pep in her steps. I watched as her thick ass switched hard. I licked my lips watching until I could no longer see her anymore.

"Nigga, get in the damn car." Keifon said causing me to chuckle as I sank down into the seat.

"Don't talk shit."

"Aye, not my fault you got it bad and haven't hit yet."

He was right. I got it bad over ol' girl. I decided that tonight I would ask her out on an official first date.

Chapter 4

Jenday

I spent a few hours in the mall purchasing a few things for myself, my sister, and my Dad. He was at the house spending time with Leah. He's been home for over a week; longer than he was usually there. I was glad about that. Leah needed this time with our father.

I pulled up to the house, grabbed my bags and got out the car. As soon as I walked in, I knew something was wrong. It was quiet besides the fact that I could hear Leah crying. I rolled my eyes already knowing what was wrong. But still, I headed to her bedroom. I sat the bags on her bed and sat beside where she was lying. I engulfed her in a hug consoling her.

"He left didn't he?"

She nodded her head as she said, "He got sick. He was shivering and scratching his arms and neck. He said he had to go get right and he'll be back once he did. He said he went to long without his medicine. I went to the bathroom and when I came back out, he was gone." She sat up and held onto me tightly crying against my chest. I sighed. There was nothing I could do but let her get it all out.

It took me almost an hour to calm her down. I got up and she followed me into the kitchen. I was going to fry some chicken wings, and cook potatoes and collard greens now since I had to work at the club tonight. I hated to leave her, but the bills had to get paid.

Two hours later, I was finished cooking. We talked for a while as we ate and then I had to get ready for work. I kissed her on the cheek and left out.

I was standing on stage ready for my set. When I was introduced, I got into my sexy character. Tank's remix with Trey Songz and Ty Dolla $ign, *When we Remix,* began to play. I loved this song. It was so sexual and got my point across.

I love the way you fuck me
But you don't understand its way more than fucking...

My body moved fluently to the beat. I thrust my hips, popped my ass, and felt up on my body. I searched the crowd for a certain face. I smirked as I saw it. Keifon had his hands on his lap as he gazed at me.

When we, fuck...

When we, fuck...

I motioned for him to come to the stage. This wasn't a part of my act, but I couldn't help myself. I dragged a chair from the corner of the stage and had him sit down. The crowd was going crazy. I placed my hands on the floor and did a handstand as I rolled my hips giving him a full very of my ass.

"Shit." I heard him say over the music. I lowered my pussy on his lap and sat up straight. His hands went to my hips as I gave him a lap dance. I stood up turning face him standing between his legs. I leaned down and whispered the lyrics to the chorus of the song. He reached around and smack my ass with his eyes on me. I continued to sexily dance on and around him until the song was over and I disappeared behind the curtain with the wink of my eye.

"Girrrrrl, you showed out tonight. I don't know how I'm going to top that shit." Princess, one of the other dancers stated. She goes on after me, and I must say, my act will be a tough one to follow.

"You got this girl. You still going to make bank." I smiled and walked around her to my dressing room. James came in handing me my money as always with lust in his eyes. He didn't say anything. All he did was hand me my money and leave. I frowned because I had no idea what that was about.

"Jenday, I have a request for you in a private room. I told him you don't entertain that way, but he insisted. He says his name is Keifon. If you want him to leave, I'll have security kick him out." The Club's manager, Walt came in and said.

I shook my head saying, "I'll go, but only for him. Don't make it a habit."

He nodded and left. We had rooms upstairs in which we can entertain. Most times, men just want an escape from their wives or girlfriends. As far as I know, it's no sex or anything like that. Just conversations and maybe a dance.

I was sure to use my wipes and freshen up. I didn't want to be in his presence with a musty pussy or armpits. I grabbed my bag and headed out of the dressing room.

"He's in room three." Walt informed me and I made my way upstairs.

I opened the door and he was sitting there looking delicious with a glass of dark liquor in his hand. His eyes moved down my body before meeting my eyes.

"Baby, I don't even know what to say. You are mad talented." He shook his head like he was in disbelief.

I sat beside him with my right leg up against the couch facing him. I took him in for a few seconds before saying, "Thank you. Now why did you want to see me? The last time, you were out of here as soon as my set was over.

He shrugged his shoulder saying, "Afraid of rejection, I guess. You seem to have a better attitude towards me. What changed?"

"Probably because you aren't acting like an asshole." I chortled causing him to do the same.

"My bad about that. Honestly, I'm used to women letting me talk to them any kind of way. I see you aren't that way. That shit turns me on too. A strong-minded woman that knows what she wants, and what she's not going for."

I simply smiled as I gazed into his dark hypnotizing eyes. We didn't say anything for a few minutes letting the music entertain us. He seemed down though, and I had to know why, so I asked.

He huffed as he stated, "My brother was shot a few days ago."

"Oh my God, is he okay?"

"He is out of the hospital, but I'm still worried about him. I just keep thinking, what if he didn't make it."

"Hey…" I placed my hand on his shoulder and continued to say, "Don't think like that. He is okay, and that's what matters now."

He nodded agreeing with me as he took a sip of his drink. He rested it against his knee and said, "Listen, I need to get home. I just wanted a moment of your time and tell you that I enjoyed your show. I'm feeling you like crazy. You cool peoples from what I can tell. Let me get your number, I wouldn't mind getting to know you a lil' bit."

"Okay."

"For real?" He sat up straight. I guess he thought I would decline his request.

"Why not. There is nothing wrong with meeting new friends." He pulled out his phone handing it to me. I entered my number and when I gave it back, he called my phone. I pulled it out locking his number in before it rang.

"You got a man calling you this late?" He asked. I shook my head as I answered.

"Hey."

"Where are you Jenday? You should be home by now."

"I'm sorry sis, I saw a friend and was running my mouth. I'm on my way though. Is there food left?"

"Yes, see you when you get here." Leah then hung up.

"That's my sister. I'm pretty much her guardian. She is at home alone, so I have to get going." I stood up.

"How old is she?"

"Sixteen."

"Damn Ma, where are your parents?"

"My mom died and my dad is on drugs and ain't shit. I have to go though, call me and we'll talk."

He stood up and we stood awkwardly until he grabbed me briefly giving me a hug. When he pulled away, we both walked out the room and headed outside separating going to our cars. He made me promise to call him when I got home and I agreed.

******

A week later

I had a full day off and I promised Leah that I would get her hair done. We had just pulled up to the hair salon when my phone rang.

"Hello."

"What's up, Jenday."

It was Keifon. He and I have been talking on the phone for the past few days. We haven't seen each other because we've been busy. I shot a video yesterday with another local artist.

"Hey, Keifon."

Leah's head snapped towards me with a frown. I know what she was thinking. She remembers what I said about him and was wondering why I was speaking with him. I smiled at her motioning for her to get out the car.

"What you up too, lady?"

"I'm about to walk in the salon with my sister, can I call you back?"

"Yea, but I'd rather see you. Let me take you out or something tonight. You off right?"

"Yes, I'm off, and we can do that. I will call you when I get my sister back home and situated."

"Okay." He replied and we ended the call.

"I thought you weren't going to talk to him." Leah stated.

"I wasn't, but we talked at my other job. He's cool when he's not being an ass." I smiled.

"As long as you're happy." Was all she said as she shrugged her shoulders as we stepped inside the salon. Our stylist, Cyndi, got to work immediately washing my hair. Once I was under the dryer, she started on Leah's hair.

We were in the salon for a good hour by now. I was replying to Keifon's message when I heard, "That's that bitch from the video shoot. She was all up in Keifon's face, girl."

I glanced up to see the girl that Keifon talked to, or currently talks to, whichever it is. At the video shoot that day, she didn't seem important to him by the way he told her off. I smiled at her and she rolled her eyes. I wasn't going to act a fool because Leah was here with me. Her friend said something smart, but I couldn't hear what she said. I just knew it was some bullshit by the way they were laughing and carrying on. None of it bothered me though.

"Jenday, isn't that the girl from the club that was trying to talk to your new friend?" I nodded my head at Leah and she replied, "She seems mad, what are you going to do if she tries to fight you. If you want to fight, that's okay. I will take her friend because I'm not letting them jump you."

I chuckled replying to her, "I am not going to fight unless she puts her hands on me. She is mad for no reason, I don't even know him like that. She can talk shit all she wants too. I have something for her." I lifted my phone and sent Keifon a message telling him what was going on. I then placed my phone in my lap and glared at her.

"What the fuck you looking at?"

"You, making a fool of yourself for a man that doesn't even want you."

"You don't know what he wants."

"I know what the fuck I saw. And by the way he was trying to holla at me in front of you, lets me know that you aren't shit to him. Now, I am spending time with my little sister right now. There is no point of me whipping your ass since I barely know him." I sat back not saying anything else. Her and her friend got hype and Cyndi told them that they had to leave if they don't calm down.

"Nah, Cyndi, she talking shit," Prissy replied.

"Girl, you came up in here trying her. If it were me it wouldn't have been no talking, but I see she is on her grown woman, and that's okay." One of the other stylist replied.

"I don't care. She trying to take my man."

The shop erupted in laughter as one of the patrons said, "You trippin' Prissy. If what she said is true, you are mad for no damn reason. Who you need to be mad at is that nigga. He is the one that approached her. Never get mad at the woman because I'm sure that she didn't know shit about you. That's what's wrong with women today. Always want to blame the other woman." The lady shook her head. The other ladies in the shop agreed with her. Still, I sat there not saying anything. There was no need. These ladies told her what I was thinking.

"Fuck that. Y'all don't know shit." She angrily spat as she inched towards me. I wasn't going to move an inch, but if she touches me, I'm going to bitch slap her ass. I don't play that disrespectful shit. Especially over a guy that I've only seen twice and only been talking to a few days. Shit, me and Keifon haven't done anything but hug. She trippin', trippin'. When she was close enough to reach out and touch me, the door chimed alerting us that someone entered the shop.

"If you touch her, I am going to toss you across this room!"

I smirked watching her eyes widen at the sound of Keifon's voice. The ladies in the shop chuckled. I'm sure it was because he came up in there defending me, and not her when she claimed that

Keifon was her man. Now everyone knew that I was indeed telling the truth.

"Oomph."

"Ooo."

"I guess we see she was telling the truth." Were some of the comments from the ladies. I smirked, winking my eye at Prissy as Keifon walked towards me and kneeled at me feet. He placed his hands on my knees and I felt an electric shock through my body at his touch

"You good?"

"Yes, I am. I need to go ahead and tell you that I am not putting up with this shit. We are only friends, and if it becomes more, I can't imagine how things will be. Set her straight or don't even call me anymore. If I have to get my hands dirty, it will be all bad for her." I rolled my eyes. This shit was low-key embarrassing.

Nah, J, you don't even have to do all that. Can I get a kiss?" He smirked. Normally, I wouldn't do it, but since I knew he was trying to prove a point, I lifted the dryer from my head and leaned in with my lips puckered. He met me halfway and pecked my lips three times.

"I'm sorry. I will handle it." He pecked my lips once more. Ooo's and Ahh's were heard throughout the salon as I smiled and winked my eye at Prissy again. I was taunting her knowing she wasn't going to attempt anything. Not in front of Keifon anyway.

"Really Keifon. You really choosing this new bitch over me..." Prissy's voice trembled. She has it bad for a man that isn't interested in her. Even Stevie Wonder could see he didn't want her ass.

"Aye, watch your fucking mouth. This is not what you do. What did I tell you would happen if you got out of pocket again?"

Prissy glanced down at the floor. When she lifted her head she had tears in her eyes as she stated, "That you would cut me off."

"Exactly, so you know what it is." He turned back to me and said, "I'll see you tonight, right?"

"I can't wait."

"Ahhight, see you later then." He gently touched my jaw with the back of his hand before standing, and walking out of the salon while the ladies whispered and made jokes about Prissy. Even her friend was shaking her head. She must be scared of him or something because all she did was turn on her heels and storm out of the salon without getting her hair done.

I turned to Leah and said, "That's how you handle a delusional bitch."

Keifon

Prissy is out of her mind. When Jenday texted me to inform me that Prissy was in the salon talking shit, I asked for the address and was one way. I don't know what made Prissy think that she could act out of character and still be in my life. We haven't ever been on that level. She has always known that we were only fucking. The bitch must have caught feelings, and that's not my problem. I heard her footsteps before I even heard her voice.

"Keifon, please."

I kept walking until I was at my car. She reached out touching my arm and I snatched away.

"I don't understand, why are you trying to talk to other people, we were doing good."

"Prissy, man…" I raked my hand down my face and continued to say, "I have never even took you out on a date. I even told you that we are only fuck buddies. You caught feelings, I didn't. So since you cant handle it, I am going to need you to fall back."

"You know what, you are going to miss me when I'm gone." She switched off as I laughed at her ass. I got in my car and pulled off.

I pulled up to my parent's house. I wanted to check on Orion. I haven't spoken to him in a day. I know he was losing his mind at our parents house. We love our mother to death, but she can be overbearing at times. And I know she over doing it considering he was shot.

The front door was open, so I walked in making my presence known.

"Hey, Ma." I sat down on the couch beside her kissing her temple.

"Hey, baby." She smiled at me.

"Where your husband and son?"

"Your Dad is at work and Orion is out back."

Right when she said it, Orion walked into the living room.

"What's up, bro?" I spoke as he made his way over to my giving me dap before sitting down. He was still moving a little slow. I will be glad when he's at one hundred percent. We needed to get these other cars soon. I'm ready to get this shit over with.

"I'm good, bro," he replied.

We sat around talking with my mother for a bit. Then we excused ourselves headed upstairs to his old bedroom.

"Man, I was thinking. We can still do that. I can be the driver. The sooner we get this done, the sooner we be out and get this money."

"Are you sure?"

"Yea, I'm good."

"Ahhight." I pulled out my phone texting Bizo to let him know.

I waited a few seconds and he texted me back.

"Bizo said he spotted the second and third cars. He says that we can get them both done in a few days."

"That's what's up."

We planned it out before I let him know I had to leave. I said my goodbye's to him and my mother before going home. I had to shower and get dressed for my date.

******

Jenday texted me her address an hour ago. I pulled up in her driveway and got out the car making my way to her door. I knocked and waited for her to answer. When the door opened, it was her sister.

"Hey, lil' lady. Where's your sister?"

"She is still getting dressed. You can come in." She stepped back allowing me to enter. I made my way to the couch sitting down.

"I hope you are serious about my sister. She has been through so much and deserve to be happy. I would hate to fight you," her sister said.

I smirked at her little ass. I respected her for what she said. I could tell that she really loves her sister, which was understandable considering Jenday was currently the only guardian she had.

"I respect that, lil' lady. You don't have to worry about me messing up. I'm feeling your sister for real," I replied.

She nodded her head as Jenday walked up front.

"Damn," I whispered. She looked good as fuck. She was wearing the hell out of a black dress that stopped at her knees, and hugged her body. She was wearing a pair of black stiletto sandals showing off her pretty ass toes that were painted pink. Her hair had a part down the middle framing her beautiful face. I stood up making my way to her. I placed my arms around her saying, "You look good, baby."

She blushed as she replied, "Thank you. You look handsome yourself." She then turned to her sister and said, "Alright Leah, you know the drill. Don't go anywhere and don't open the door for anyone. I'm not sure where we are going, but if you want something to eat other than what's in the kitchen, just call and let me know. Come lock up."

"Okay sis, have fun." She stood up and followed us to the door. After we stepped out, Jenday stood there until she heard the locks click.

We made our way to my royal blue Camaro with black racing strips on the hood. I opened the door for her and she got in. Once she was situated, I shut the door and rounded the front getting into the drivers seat.

"Where are we going? I am starving."

"I wanted to try that restaurant everyone is talking about. Steak 48. That's cool with you?"

"Yes, sounds great."

I backed out of her driveway and headed to Sharon road. The ride was silent at first until we were on the highway. I couldn't stand the silence so I let her know, "Aye, I love the way you are taking care of your little sister. That shit is admirable."

"Thank you." She turned towards me and smiled.

"I really have no choice. Like I was telling you the other night, my mom passed away. She got in a car accident the night after my high school graduation. My Dad was already on drugs which was why my mother was out late. She had to have two jobs to take care of the house. After she passed, my Dad got worse. He will be gone for weeks at a time. I have no idea where he be. All I know is he be getting high. He comes home sometimes to wash his ass and get a delicious meal. Every time he leaves, my sister is a mess. He came home and stayed for a little over a week and left three days ago."

"Damn, baby. I'm sorry to hear that. At least she has you."

"Yea." We were silent again. I guess we both were in our own thoughts. Twenty-four minutes later, we were pulling up to the restaurant. I got out, opened her door then placed my hand possessively on her lower back leading her into the restaurant.

"Good evening, table for two?"

"Yes, I called in a reservation for Keifon."

"Got you. Right this way." The hostess led us to our table. When she walked off our waitress walked right up. We ordered our drinks. I ordered a glass of Hennessey and coke, and she ordered a fruity mixed drink. We also ordered Lobster rolls as an appetizer.

We scanned the menu figuring out what we wanted to eat. She placed her menu down first. I glanced up at her once I had decided what I wanted and asked, "So what's your story, baby? You seem like you've been through a lot."

She sat up in her seat intertwining her fingers on the table.

"Well, I am twenty-four. Right now I should be on Broadway. I had a full scholarship to Julliard, but when that tragedy happened with my mother, I decided that I needed to turn it down to care for my sister. It was an easy decision, I wouldn't have dared left her in my Dad's care."

"Damn, I hate that for you."

The waitress appeared placing our drinks on the table along with our Lobster rolls. We then placed our orders before she took our menu's and stepped away to go put our orders in. She lifted a lobster roll taking a bite before placing it on a plate.

"This is good." She licked a crumb off her lip drawing my attention to those juicy things. I then tasted one and agreed with her.

"You are a strong ass selfless woman, baby. I admire that about you. I hate you had to alter your life. And you are doing what you have to do to take care of your sister. At eighteen, I know that was a lot."

She nodded her head and I noticed her getting teary eyed. I reached over placing my hand on top of hers.

"Hey, why are you crying?"

"It's just that sometimes I feel like I'm not doing enough. To hear you say that I am strong tugs at my heart."

"You are strong, baby. Keep doing what you're doing. Let's change the subject, I hate to see these tears."

She nodded as she smiled and said, "Okay, tell me about you then. What do you do for a living?"

I wasn't going to tell her everything but enough.

"I own a club and an underground gambling spot."

"Oh. How does that work?"

"The gambling spot is connected to our club. No one knows it's there unless you know someone that has been there. We charge a monthly fee to be able to gamble. It's a great hustle. My club is also exclusive. It's the club that Bizo's video shoot was at."

"Oh wow. You are going to have to take me there on a regular night. I want to see this gambling spot too."

"I can do that." Right then. The waitress came and sat our food on the table.

"Do you guys need anything else right now?"

"I will take another drink," I replied.

"I will too," said Jenday.

"Alright, I will be right back."

My steak and her lamb chops looked delicious. I heard Jenday moan as she took her first bite.

"Don't do that." I Smirked. That moan sounded sexy as hell.

"What?"

"All that damn moaning." I chuckled.

"Shit, this steak is good. Taste yours."

I cut a piece off and slid it into my mouth. She was right, this shit was juicy and tender.

"You're right. I guess the restaurant lives up to the hype."

"Yes it does."

We spent a few minutes eating in silence. After we got a fill from the food, we conversed about any and everything. She was actually good company. Nothing like when I first met her. I think we will be great friends, hopefully that will turn into more.

We didn't have room for desert, so I asked for the check, paid and we left.

Back in the car, we continued our conversation. I didn't want to take her home, but I knew she had her sister, so I wasn't trippin'.

We pulled up to her house and sat in the car. She didn't make a move to get out and I didn't either. We sat in silence for a while. I am feeling this girl like hell. She seems to fit me well.

"How is your brother doing?"

See, shit like that makes me like her even more. She didn't have to ask about my brother, she doesn't even know him.

"He's doing good. Getting better by the day. I just saw him earlier."

"That's good to hear."

I opened my door and got out then walked to her side letting her out.

"You trying to get rid of me?" She questioned.

I shut her door pushing her up against the car standing in front of her with my hands on her hips.

"Nah, I just felt the need to touch you." I stepped closer so that our bodies were touching.

She blushed lowering her head to the ground. I lifted it with my finger making her look at me.

"Don't be shy, baby. I love staring at your beautiful face." She smiled wide placing her hands around my neck pulling me even closer.

"I want to kiss you so bad."

She didn't say anything. Instead, she leaned in placing her lips against mine. I used my tongue to part her lips with my hand on the back of her head deepening the kiss. My damn dick was rising by the second. I had to pull away. When I did, she had a smirk on her face.

"Yea, you do that to me," I replied. She bit her lip and pulled me back to her for another kiss. This time she lifted her leg placing it around my waist. I lifted her body so that her back was against my car and both her legs were around me. I could feel the heat from her pussy since she had on a dress and it rose to her waist.

"Mmm." She moaned into my mouth. Her hips were moving trying to feel my dick and I let her. I moved my hand to her thigh moving it up to her panties rubbing over the seat of her panties. She didn't stop me so I continued and moved my hand inside her panties. I felt that her pussy was smooth as hell. I strummed her clit as we continued to kiss.

"Damn, baby. This pussy wet." I slid my finger into her pussy moving it in and out slowly. She thrust her hips in sync with my fingers. Her eyes closed momentarily with her mouth hanging open. Shit was sexy as fuck.

"Damn," I whispered feeling her get wetter. I wanted to get up in her so bad, but I had a feeling she wasn't going for it. I slid a second finger into her and felt her pussy clinch. Her mouth formed an O, as she came. I attached my lips to hers kissing nastily as she came down from her orgasmic high. When I pulled away and removed my fingers from her pussy, I slid them into my mouth.

"Damn this shit is good. Taste," I demanded. She opened her mouth and I put my fingers between us as we both got a taste. We kissed a few seconds longer before I removed her legs from around me letting her feet touch the ground.

"I needed that," she whispered.

"I got more if you want."

She shook her head saying, "We are not ready for that yet."

"Respect," I simply replied.

"You going to have me gone girl. Go on in the house. I will holla at you tomorrow." I leaned in pecking her lips. I then stood there until she was safely inside the house. I shook my head getting myself together before getting in my car and pulling off.

Chapter 5

Oba

It was a busy night and I am tired as I don't know what. The good thing about it is that this was my last week working the night shift for a minute. We have a few new hires that need to be trained and my supervisor thought that I would be perfect for the job.

I was gathering my things in the nurses room when my phone pinged alerting me of a text. I lifted my phone seeing that it was Orion. I smiled as I sat on the bed that was there for us to get some rest to reply to him.

Orion: I can't wait to see you later.

Really? Why you want to see me?

Orion: I always want to see your sexy ass.

All I need is a few hours of sleep and I will be good to go. Is six or seven this evening good?

That would be perfect because that will give me all day to get some sleep.

Orion: Perfect baby.

I stood up placing my bag on my shoulder leaving to say my goodbye's to Brittany and a few other staff members before heading out.

What are we going to do?

I texted him back as I was exciting the elevator on the bottom floor to get to the parking deck.

Orion: It's whatever. As long as I'm with you.

Are you feeling okay to go out? Are your wounds hurting?

Orion: I'm good baby. Not like we are going to be doing anything strenuous.

Okay.

I was in the process of typing something else when my phone was snatched out of my hand. I cursed as I looked up seeing Tommy glaring at me with hatred in his eyes.

"Who the fuck making you smile like that?" He seethed.

My phone was steady pinging. I struggled with him to get my phone back.

"Give me my damn phone, Tommy. You are not my man. You are nothing to me."

He held my phone high up in the air so that I couldn't reach it. He then turned his back continuously pushing me back so that I couldn't get to it. He was reading the messages. When he finished, he slung my phone against the concrete wall causing it to fall to the ground in pieces.

"What is wrong with you? I'm glad I left you alone."

"Who is that nigga? Is that the nigga who answered your phone? The one you were all up on when you pushed him out the hospital? That's not even a part of your job description. You fucking patients now?" He cocked his head to the side. I didn't want to hear any of that. I tried to walk away but he snatched me back.

"Aye, get your hands off the lady." Hospital security was rushing towards us with his hand on his gun.

Tommy stepped away with his hands up. He smirked at me as he said, "I'll be seeing you." He then turned and walked away.

"Are you good Miss?"

"Yes, thank you." I turned around picking up my broken phone hoping that it could be fixed. It couldn't. Now I'm mad that I will have to spend money on another phone. I made my way to my car getting in and headed home so that I could call Orion from the house phone. I'm sure he has texted me a few times wondering why I wasn't responding. I can't believe Tommy. I can see now that he is going to be a problem. I don't have time for shit like this. He is the reason why I don't want a boyfriend now. They are too much trouble.

Honestly, I don't even know why I'm wasting my time with Orion. I unintentionally smiled. Then again, I know exactly why. He doesn't seem like other men that I have met or dated. He seems, cool, real, and down to earth. Then the fact that he is so fucking fine.

I pulled up to my house and glanced around the street making sure that Tommy's crazy ass didn't come here. I didn't see anything out of the ordinary, so I got out of my car and hurriedly went inside. I locked the door before going to my bedroom.

The first thing I did was throw my hair into a messy bun and tied a silk scarf around it. I removed my shoes before sitting on the bed.

I dialed Orion's number from my memory and waited for him to answer.

"Fuck is this?"

"Damn, that's how you answer the phone?" I chuckled.

"Hell yea, I didn't know who you were. Who's phone is this, baby?"

I sighed before letting him know that this was my house number. He proceeded to ask me what was wrong with my phone? And when I told him, he was livid. You would have though that I was his woman.

"He didn't follow you home and shit did he?"

"No, but it's not like he doesn't know where I live."

"What's your address baby. I don't even want you there by yourself right now."

"Orion, I'm fine. Plus, I am only going to fall asleep on you."

"That's cool. I'll chill and watch TV or some shit."

I thought about it for a second. I didn't mind him coming over, and I trusted him. After I gave him my address he asked, "You had an iPhone or android?"

Not thinking anything of it, I told him, "I had the Galaxy s10."

"Cool, I'll be there in a few. Gone in there and wash that bangin' body."

I blushed as I told him that I'd see him when he got here. I placed the cordless phone back on the base and undressed on my way to the bathroom. I turned on the shower letting it get hot while I placed my shower cap over my head. Afterwards, steam was coming from the shower, so I stepped in. I thoroughly washed myself before getting out.

I massaged body butter into my skim before slipping on a pair of boy shorts, and a tank top. Yea, I'm being fast, but I'm grown. Plus, it's not like I can hide all this ass anyway.

I glanced at the time on my cable box seeing that forty minutes have passed and he wasn't here yet. I made my way to my kitchen to cook my something quick to eat.

"Shit, I need to go grocery shopping," I said to myself as I looked in the refrigerator. I pulled out the pack of bacon, the mayonnaise, lettuce, tomato, and an onion. I grabbed a frying pan from the cabinet placing it on the stove letting it heat up. Once it was hot, I placed slices of bacon in it for my BLT sandwich. I wasn't sure if he had eaten, but I was going to fix one for him, too. I spread mayo on the bread then built the rest of the sandwich waiting on the bacon to cook.

Hearing the doorbell ring, I walked to the door being sure to stand on my toes to look through the peephole. When I was sure that it was Orion, and not Tommy, I opened the door.

"Hey." I allowed him to walk in.

"What's up. You cooking bacon?"

"Yea, I wasn't sure if you had eaten, but I'm making you a BLT too."

"Shiiit, that's perfect. I haven't eaten shit since last night."

It was only ten in the morning, so that was normal. He followed me to the kitchen and sat on a stool.

"I'm feeling your décor. Your place is nice. It fits you," he let me know.

I had a lot of African artwork on my walls, and my home was decorated in earthly tones.

"Thank you." I took the last of the bacon out of the pan letting the grease drain on a napkin. I then finished making the sandwiches before sliding a plate towards him.

"Thanks. I appreciate this shit. Come over here, I got something for you."

I lifted my plate rounding the counter and sat beside him. He handed me a T-Mobile bag. I know this man didn't buy me a phone.

"What's this?"

"Open it," he demanded and I did.

"Oh wow. You got me the Galaxy 21? How much did you pay. I can go to the bank and get your money."

He shook his head while saying, "You good, Oba. I just couldn't let you go without a phone for no amount of days. I need to be able to talk to you at all times."

I placed the box in front of me and took a bite of my sandwich. After I swallowed it, I asked, "Are you sure?"

"Yup."

We ate our food in silence. By the time I was finished with my food, I was yawning.

"Gone and get some sleep. I can clean the kitchen. You mind if I smoke in here?"

"You don't have to do that."

"I know, but you're tired and I can see you keep your house spotless, so let me handle this."

"Okay, and yes you can smoke in here. Just get a plastic cup and put a little bit of water in it for your ashes. I don't have an ashtray."

"I can do that." He licked his lips as his eyes fell on my body.

I chuckled as I walked away headed to my bedroom. My pillow was calling my damn name.

******

I woke up to a hand on my ass. I glanced over my shoulder seeing Orion asleep next to me. He had his shirt off and was only in his basketball shorts. I admired his body. It was looking right. His muscular chest, and his abs...ooo lord.

I didn't want to move because for some reason, his strong hand on my ass was comforting. His hand was soft like he hasn't done any arduous work in his life.

"You just going to stare at a nigga?"

I giggled as I turned completely around. He didn't move his hand from my body, but it sat against my hip.

"When did you come in here?"

"After I cleaned up the kitchen, and smoked a blunt. A nigga was tired and your bed is way more comfortable than your couch."

"Well I'm glad you took your shirt off. Don't want my bed smelling like weed."

"Oh nah, I know better."

We gazed into each other's eyes until I asked, "Tell me about yourself Orion. I have you all in my house and don't know anything about you."

"Lets see...I have one brother, Keifon. He is my stepbrother, but we close as hell. Our parents got together when we were younger. I own a club and a little gambling spot. It's illegal, so don't go telling people." He chuckled.

"I wouldn't do that," I let him know.

"I am twenty-six. And I am feeling you." He finished then asked about me. I ran down my life story to him as I checked the time. It was five o'clock already.

"I love that you got a good head on your shoulders. That's some sexy shit."

"Do you have a woman, Orion?"

"Nah, I have women that get me off when I need it, but you are in my life now. They all cut off."

I smacked my teeth as I said, "Yea right." I rolled my eyes.

"Dead ass. You know, my momma told me that you wouldn't take my shit, and I took heed to her words."

"I hear you," I replied. We stared at each other again. The next thing I knew, he was leaning in for a kiss. It started as a peck, then it was so passionate and sensual that my pussy purred. I had to pull back before I did something that we weren't ready for.

"I've been wanting to do that since I saw you in my hospital room."

I blushed, because honestly, I felt the same way. His hand moved up and down my hip. He asked, "What you want to do tonight?"

"I really don't feel like getting dressed to go out. I want to be around you though. We can order out and watch a movie or something."

"We can do that," he agreed. We lay there and talked for at least another hour getting to know each other. He was funny as hell, had me cracking up.

By seven o'clock, we were laying in my bed eating Chinese food and watching a hood movie on Prime. I was having a good as time being around him. He seems like a good dude. Lets just hope he was showing his true self and not wearing a mask.

Orion

Oba is cool as shit. I'm kind of glad she decided to stay in. It gave me a chance to fill her out. I'm usually a good judge of character, and from this one day, I can tell that she was a different breed.

I was dead ass when I told her that it was all about her now. I had my head laying on her legs watching this movie. I could smell her arousal, but I kept myself in check. Unless she makes the first move, I won't do anything.

My phone rang and I sat up to answer it. It was Bizo saying that he needed to speak to me and he's on his way to the gambling spot. I hung up the phone and told Oba, "Ride with me somewhere. I need to handle some business and I'm not ready for our night to end."

"Where are we going?"

"To my gambling spot. I need to meet someone there for a minute. Then I can give you a tour of the club, and shit while we're there."

"Okay." She agreed as she got out of the bed and walked into her closet to get some clothes to put on. She came back a few minutes later in a pair of jeans that hugged her hips, and a fitted t-shirt showing those big ass breast of hers. She removed her bonnet, but kept her hair up in a messy bun. She pulled on a pair of Jordan's then grabbed her purse, the new phone a purchased for her, and her keys saying that she was ready. I already had my shirt and shorts on, so I grabbed her hand and we headed out the door.

We pulled up to my club in no time. I got out then let her out. She fell in stride with me as we made our way inside the club. It was only nine at night, therefore, only the workers were there.

I didn't see Bizo's truck out front, so I went ahead and showed her around the club part.

"This is nice, Orion." The smile on her face was beautiful.

"Thank you. This belongs to my brother and me. You remember him from the hospital right?"

"I do," she replied.

"You want a drink?" I asked her.

"Yea, I can use one." I instructed her to sit at the bar while I went behind it to fix her a drink.

"Hey, Orion." Lucky smiled stepping close to me like she didn't see me with a woman.

"What's good, Luck. Step back." The frown she wore on her face faded as she glanced into the smiling face of Oba.

"Hey." Oba wiggled her fingers, not in the least bit worried about Lucky's ass. I chuckled as I asked Oba what she wanted to drink.

"A little vodka, it doesn't matter what kind. With Cranberry juice and a splash of orange juice."

I busied myself fixing her drink and myself a cup of Hennessey and Coke. I stepped back around the bar grabbing her handing making our way to the gambling spot.

"Oh, so it's connected?"

"Yes, no one ever suspects it's here. You have to know the code to get in and buy in is one-thousand dollars. If you can't afford it, you don't get in."

"That's smart. It cuts down on people trying to snitch. Most people think it's like VIP or some shit."

"What's good Orion? You working tonight?" James asked. James is the manager of the Club. He is a solid dude and runs a tight ship. Keifon and I rarely have to come here because he does his thing. When we are here, we are mostly next door.

"Nah, I came to meet Keifon and Bizo, then I'm headed out."

"That's what's up." He moved his eyes to Oba raking his eyes down her body.

"Who is this?"

"Mine, nigga. You cool, but fucking with her will get you hurt." I warned.

He held his hands up in surrender saying, "My bad bro. Just never seen you step in here with a woman. I wasn't going to disrespect her."

"As long as you know. Let them know I'm over here when they fall through."

"Got'cha." James walked off.

"I am not yours, buddy." I heard Oba say from beside me.

"Yet."

"Hun." She frowned.

"You are not mine, yet." I raised my eyebrow daring her to deny it.

She shook her head as I led her around the room seeing the different tables and machines.

"This is set up nicely. I would think I'm in a legit casino."

"That is kind of the point. Come sit over here with me." She followed me and was about to take a seat beside me, but I pulled her onto my lap. She smiled at me with the gorgeous smile of hers. This woman was so damn fine. I reached up pushing a piece of her hair back that fell in her face.

"I love your hair." I leaned forward sniffing it.

"It smells good as fuck too. What do you put in it?"

"Just a few oils." She shrugged.

"That's what's up."

I saw Bizo walking up and I told Oba that I would be right back. I walked off to see what this nigga wanted. I listened to what he had to say. All I said back was, "Ahhight, we got it. I'm going to holla at you though. I'm here with my, lady."

"That's cool." We slapped hands and then I joined Oba. We chilled at the club for another hour before we left and I took her home. I had some business to handle tonight, otherwise, I would have stayed with her. She seemed upset about it, but I promised to see her the next day.

.

Chapter 6

Keifon

It is Saturday and the day we decided to boost two cars. We were trying to get this shit over with. Orion and I were already risking shit having the gambling spot. Our father said we should think about going through the process of having a legal gambling spot. We were thinking on it. Then Bizo's music career is starting to take off and he doesn't need to be wrapped up in this shit. To him, he was only doing it to pay for studio time, and videos.

We already unloaded the first car which was a McClaren. That one went off without a hitch.

"Aye, y'all sure you want to get the third car tonight?" Puma seemed concerned.

"Yea man, we good."

"Ahhight then, switch cars. I don't want y'all seen in the same car you used to get the other one." He lifted a set of keys from his drawer and handed them to me saying, "It's a black Oldsmobile around back. Take that one." He reached into his drawer pulling out a set of keys.

"Y'all know what to do in the event that you get caught right?" Puma glared at us with a pointed look.

"That's why we won't get caught. If by chance…we know to do our time. It's all good, bro." Orion stated and then we walked out the shop headed around back. We got in the car and Orion pulled off. I didn't trust for him to help steal the car since technically, he was still recovering from getting shot last time.

The Bentley that we are going to get was parked in the parking deck of a high-rise condo downtown. This should be easy as long as no one is around.

"Ahhight, y'all ready?"

"Let's do this. Orion, when we get out, turn the car around and come back right here."

Bizo and I got out the car and did our thing quickly. It took no time to turn that alarm off and considering it was in a parking deck, even if someone inside heard the alarm. It would take a minute for them to get down to where we were.

Bizo eased out of the parking deck turning onto the street with me and Orion behind him. We were gone for an hour before pulling back up to the shop. Bizo pulled the car into the bay as Orion parked in the back.

We walked into Puma's office and he was surprised to see us back so soon.

"Okay fellas, you are halfway done. Here..." He slid a bag across his desk.

"What's this?" I inquired.

"One point five. You will get the other half when I get the other three cars."

Shit, I wasn't expecting that, but it was cool with me. We left and went back to my house where Orion and Bizo parked their car. We then went inside to split the money before they left me alone.

I took a shower before winding down with a blunt, and a glass of dark liquor. I was sitting on my back porch when Jenday crossed my mind and I decided to call her. It was late as shit, but I wanted to talk to her regardless. I haven't seen her since I dropped her off after our date and I needed to hear her voice.

"Hello." She answered the phone with sleep filled voice sounding sexy as fuck.

"I woke you up?"

"Yes, you did. But it's fine."

"How was your day?" I slumped down further into my chair focusing on the conversation.

"It was cool. Leah wanted to go shopping of course, so we went to a boutique downtown. That girl can shop."

"She probably gets it from her big sister."

"Probably." She giggled.

There was a few moments of silence before she asked, "What are you doing up this time of night?"

"Shit, smoking so I can get some sleep. I wish I were over there with you."

Silence. I had to pull the phone away from my ear to make sure she was there.

"You feel like driving?"

"If I'm coming to you, hell yea."

"Come on."

"I'm on my way." We disconnected our call and I was hype at this point. I hurriedly put my blunt out and headed back in the house. I took a quick shower and dressed in basketball shorts, a t-shirt, and slides. I also packed me a bag with an outfit for tomorrow. I was out the door in record time.

Jenday opened the door speaking after I rang her doorbell.

"Hey," she greeted me.

"What's good," I replied giving her a hug before she shut and locked the door, and then set the alarm.

She walked ahead of me to the back of the house where we entered her bedroom.

"Did you already shower?"

"Yes."

"Okay." She got in her bed under the covers. I removed my shirt laying on the foot of the bed. When she glanced up at me with her lip damn near touching the floor I smirked.

"You liking what you see?" I knew a nigga was built. She over there salivating at the mouth and shit. She snapped out of it playing it off saying, "Boy, ain't nobody looking at you."

"Boy…" I lifted my eyebrow. I wasn't all the way in the bed yet, so I stood up straight. With my eyes on her, I hooked my fingers inside my shorts and pulled them down my legs, stepping out of them. I was wearing boxer briefs and her sight fell towards my dick like I knew it would.

"Does this look like a boy to you?" I gripped my dick so she could see the weight of it. She shook her head like she was trying to get rid of those nasty thoughts that were swimming around in that pretty little head of hers.

"Are you getting in bed or you gonna keep staring like a creep?"

I chuckled while sliding into the bed with her. The room was dark considering there wasn't a TV or anything on. Her back was facing me, but I didn't like that. I gently pressed down on her shoulder instructing her to, "Turn around." She did as I asked with a huff. That still wasn't good enough for me. She was too far away. I slid closer to her and lifting her leg placing it over mine.

"I need you near me tonight. You are like my peace. When I'm around you, everything else disappears."

"What's going on, you need to talk about it?"

"Nah, I just want to lay up under you and get some rest."

She seemed content with that answer. We didn't say anything else. She lay in my arms getting comfortable and I did the same.

Jenday

I woke up well before Keifon. Last night when he called, I don't know what came over me. But the other night when we were all over each other outside, it felt good. I wanted to feel that again.

I'm surprised I controlled myself around him. I thought I was going to be laid out spread eagle on the bed, especially when he gripped his big ass dick. That thang looked heavy and long. It was snaked down his leg.

I squeezed my legs together just thinking about it. He began to stir before his eyes popped open and he smiled.

"Good morning, Jenday."

"Good morning," I replied.

I attempted to sit up so that I could go relieve myself, but he pulled me back down.

"I'm just going to the bathroom." I giggled. He let me go and I went to handle my business before laying back down next to him.

"Yo, your sister in there cooking and shit?"

"Yea, she always knocks on my door when she's finished if I haven't come out yet."

He nodded his head as he lay on his back and pulled me on top to straddle his waist. He placed his hand on the back of my head and pulled me down for a kiss. I felt his dick rising prompting me to jump off his lap.

"Girl, what the hell wrong with you? Don't tell me you're a virgin or some shit. Not the way you be moving that body." He sat up.

I narrowed my eyes at him then chortled. "I'm not a virgin, it's just..." I took a deep breath.

"What is it?" He frowned.

"It's been a minute and I don't want to just give it up to the first guy that I am attempting to get to know. I'm not sure where this is going, and I need to be sure. I mean, so far you are a great guy, but these days, you just don't know." I sat there facing him as his facial expressions changed. I wasn't sure if that was a good, or bad thing, but if he couldn't wait a little longer, then he wasn't good for me. I don't care how cool he was nor how much I'm feeling him.

"I feel you, but I may as well let you know now that I'm going to be the one." He rubbed his hands together making the Stevie J creep face. I laughed, my head falling forward to the bed. I sat up shaking my head at his ass.

There was a knock on the door then we heard Leah's voice as she tried to open the door.

"Jenday, why is your door locked? You never lock your door. Are you okay?"

"I'm okay, Leah. We will be out in a minute."

"We, who is we, Jenday?"

"Little girl, get your hips away from my door. I'll be out." I heard her smack her teeth, but she didn't ask anymore questions.

"Damn, lil' sis acting like she the big sis." Keifon laughed as I stood up and stretched.

"Yea, she's overprotective as hell. But I am the same way about her."

"I can understand that. Me and my brother are the same way. I love how close y'all are considering what all you have lost."

I nodded my head in agreeance as I told him, "Come on before she has a fit." I stood there as he slipped his shorts and t-shirt back on, then we left my room headed towards the kitchen.

Leah was placing two plates on the table, then moved back to the stove. She was making an extra since she knew I had company. She turned back around seeing Keifon and smiled.

"Oh, hey Keifon." She then gave me the side eye.

"Good morning, baby sis."

"You can sit there." She instructed him to the plate that was beside me.

"I appreciate it. Shit looks good." Keifon stated as he sat down in his designated seat.

Leah sat down and we all dug in. I could tell she had something to say by the way her eyes kept moving to me.

She cleared her throat and asked, "So, how did this happen because the last time we were around you, my sister played you."

Keifon chuckled while replying, "Played me? Nah, her ass was playing hard to get." He glanced over at me before focusing back on his cheesy grits.

"I find that hard to believe. Jenday doesn't usually entertain men."

"Leah, I am sitting right here." I spoke up.

"Oh I know it. Just tryna figure out what changed."

"She met a real nigga," Keifon replied matter of factly.

"You better not hurt my sister Keifon, I'm not playing with you," Leah poked her lips out like her little tail can really do something to him.

I rolled my eyes. Leah was doing way too much right now. We finished up our food before I helped Leah clean the kitchen, and Keifon went onto the back porch to smoke.

"Jenday, is this a good idea?"

"Leah, I told you, he's cool. I'm the adult here, you don't have to question my decisions. I wouldn't do anything that would hurt me or you."

"But, he's going to take up a lot of your time."

I stood straight up from placing dishes in the dishwasher and asked, "Is this what all the questions are about?"

She nodded her head and I made my way over to her placing my arms around her shoulders.

"Leah, you are my sister and I love you 'til death. No one will ever come between us. He understands that. You had to know that I would meet a man someday. That in no way will take me away from my time with you. You will always be my priority." I kissed her cheek.

"You promise?"

"I promise, sis."

"Okay." She shrugged seemingly believing me. After that we finished cleaning the kitchen. Knowing how she felt, I knew I couldn't keep Keifon around all day. I chilled with him until he finished his blunt, then told him I had things to take care of today. He took a quick shower, got dressed for the day and then left. But not before giving me a big juicy kiss to think about in his absence.

Chapter 7

Oba

I was going about my day at work like usual. Seems like all I do is work these days. I need to start getting out and having fun. I was walking out of my last patient's room for the morning room when my supervisor, Nicole, approached me.

"Hey, Oba. Do you mind meeting me in my office for a second?"

"Sure thing, I'll be right there," I told her as I walked to the desk to drop off the clipboard that I was holding.

"Girl, what do you think she wants?" Brittany questioned. It was rare that Nicole asked to speak with anyone.

"I have no idea, but I guess I'm about to find out. Be right back." I headed towards the back where the offices were. I walked into her office and she instructed me to, "Have a seat."

She pecked a few keys on her keyboard before looking up at me. At this point, I didn't know what to think. I had a feeling that I wasn't going to like whatever it was she about to say.

"What is this about, you're making me nervous?" I finally spoke up.

"You are an exemplary employee. You do a phenomenal job and you are very attentive to all patients. They all love you. However, it has been brought to my attention that you have been involved with a patient. As you know that is frowned upon in this field."

My face contorted. How the hell did she know that? Several scenarios were running through my head.

"He isn't a patient anymore," I replied.

"So, then you admit it?" She raised her eyebrow.

"Nicole, I don't mean any disrespect, but my personal life is just that. But since someone wants to run their mouth about things they don't know, he and I didn't start getting to know each other until after he was discharged. I don't see what the problem is."

"I understand that, but considering someone went out of their way to bring this to my attention doesn't look good. They mentioned you started dating while he was still in the hospital."

"How is that even possible when I didn't even know him from a can of paint then? Let me get this right. I started dating a man that I do not know while he was a patient. So, three days and boom, we're together." I rolled my eyes in disbelief at the way she was coming at me. This wasn't making any sense to me so I asked, "And who did you hear this false information from?"

She glanced towards her computer screen then turned it around so that I could see it.

"It was sent anonymously."

I leaned forward to get a better look at the screen and read what was sent.

To whom it may concern,

I want to bring it to your attention a few unethical things that are going on in your hospital. One of your nurses, Oba Ibrahim has been doing things that are frowned upon. She met and began a relationship with a patient while he had been admitted into the hospital.

I find this to be disappointing that you allow nurses to carry on this way. If nothing is done about this, I will be forced to go to your higher ups.

Sincerely,

A concerned citizen

I sat back in my seat fuming. I couldn't believe this shit. It couldn't have been anyone but Tommy. He is a delusional bitch. Only bitches do shit like this.

"Because this was sent to my supervisor instead of me, I have to take action. You are suspended for one week," Nicole stated.

"What!" I exclaimed standing abruptly.

"This isn't fair. I told you what it really was and you don't believe me?" My eyes began to burn. This was something that is going to go on my permanent record.

"At this point, to them, it's about how things look. If this gets out, how will this make the hospital look?" Nicole said.

"Oh, but it's okay to have this nonsense on my record?" The first tear dropped. After that, they wouldn't stop.

"I'm sorry, Oba." She seemed sympathetic, but I didn't give a fuck.

"Yea, well fuck your sorry. I know exactly who did this.. That man is delusional and I have a feeling he is going to cause more problems in my life for the simple fact that I do not want to be with him. He choked me and I left him alone, now he is angry."

"Did you file a police report? If you did then that can help your case."

I shook my head letting her know that I did not.

"Then I have no choice. You may gather your things and return next week." She dismissed me like it was nothing. Like I was not a great asset to this hospital.. I turned and left out slamming her office door. This was some bullshit.

I went straight to the nurse's lounge and Brittany was in there gathering her things. She saw the look on my face along with my tears and asked what was wrong.

"Some straight bullshit. I'm so angry I could hurt someone. This nigga wrote an email to them talking about I am being unethical by dating Orion. We're not even dating yet." I got a napkin off the table and wiped my face.

"Who?"

"Tommy. You know I broke it off with him and he isn't happy about it."

"So, he is trying to ruin you?" She asked and I nodded.

"He's a bitch." Brittany seethed.

"Same thing I said." I shook my head as I began pulling things out of my locker.

"I am suspended for a week."

"What the fuck? Don't worry. Karma is a bitch." I agreed with her as we made our way out of the hospital. We said our goodbye's then I made my way to my car.

I crank it up, but didn't pull off right away. I was in shock. I have never gotten in trouble at work in my life. Like Nicole said, I am an exemplary employee. I don't know if she believed me or not, but the fact that she didn't fight for me was fucked up.

Now my brain was moving a mile a minute. I didn't know if it's a good idea to keep talking to Orion. I really don't see the problem with them. He was no longer a patient in that hospital. They act like I had sex with him in his hospital bed or something.

I was about to pull off when my phone rang. I glanced down seeing Tommy's number. I normally wouldn't answer, but I have a few words for him.

I pressed the green phone button to answer and said, "You are a bitch, Tommy. You are fucking with my life, and for what? Because I hurt your feelings, your little ego is bruised?"

I heard him laugh like a maniac. This man was officially crazy as fuck.

"I put in time with you, Oba. Whatever happened, you deserved that shit. You led me on making me believe that I had a future with you. You wasted my time, I could have moved on with the next bitch. Do you know how many woman want me?"

"Well go to them and leave me the fuck alone because I do not want your ass!"

"You will regret th…"

I didn't even want to hear anymore. I hung up on his ass before blocking his number. There was no reason for me to talk to him. I shook my head as I finally got myself together and pulled off.

I needed to talk to someone and didn't want to go home. I headed to my sister, Dola's house. She lived with her husband and three kids. She is six years older than me at thirty-one years old.

I pulled up to her beautiful home getting out of the car. I walked up knocking waiting on her to answer. When the door opened, my nephew, Michael answered.

"Hey auntie." He reached in hugging me, and I hugged him back. He towered over me at five feet seven. He's a tall thirteen-year-old. My sister had him young.

"Hey kiddo. What you in here doing?" I asked as I stepped inside the house allowing him to shut the door.

"In here on the game."

"Cool, where is your mom?"

"She's outside in her garden picking out her veggies. You know how she is."

"Alright, well get back to your game, I am about to go talk to her."

"Are you aright auntie? You seem upset and your eyes are red like you've been crying. Did someone break your heart, because if they did, I will beat him up."

I had to chuckle at that. My nephew was something else. I shook my head saying, "I'm okay, Michael. You don't have to beat anyone up." I rubbed his head.

"Alright." He hugged me again before turning going upstairs.

I made my way through the house to the back. I opened the sliding door and stepped out into my sisters huge backyard. I glanced back towards her garden seeing her crouched down with a hat on picking her vegetables. I saw her place a few carrots in her basket as she looked towards me.

"Hey Oba. I didn't know you were stopping by." She stood to her feet and stepped out of her little garden to hug me. I held on extra tight. I felt comfort in her arms. She pulled back first searching my face.

"What's wrong, baby sis?" Her eyes held concern. At that point, I broke down. She consoled me letting me get it all out. She led me to the bench on her back porch and we sat down.

I calmed down enough to explain what happened. She was as furious as I was.

"You mean, Tommy?" My sister and her husband met him a while back when we all went out to eat.

"I can have Paul talk to him," Dola stated.

I was already shaking my head. I didn't want my brother-in-law involved in this. Her husband was a serious man. He went hard for the one's he love. I am included in that because of my sister.

"I can't have him do that. If he does something that gets him in trouble, I won't be able to forgive myself. We both know Paul is crazy." I chuckled and so did she.

"Don't I know it."

We heard the door slide open and Paul appeared.

"What up, sis, what's going on?" He peeped our demeanor knowing something was wrong. My sister looked to me and I shrugged.

"She is having issues with Tommy because she cut him off. He chocked her and got her suspended from work."

"What the fuck!?" He stepped towards me with a frown.

"Paul, don't do anything. I can't have you getting in trouble because of me," I told him.

"I don't give a fuck about none of that shit. He violated by putting his hands on you and he is going to have to see me."

My shoulders slumped knowing that it was nothing that I could do to stop him.

"Who is this new guy, I need to meet him to make sure he is worth your time?" Dola asked.

"So far, he has been the perfect gentleman." I smiled thinking about Orion.

"What's his name?"

"Orion."

"Oh." He looked to the side then back to me and asked, "He has a brother named Keifon?"

I perked up letting him know that it was indeed him.

"I know that nigga. He's a cool cat. I've been to their gambling spot a few times. We smoked a blunt or two together. I still need to holla at him though. He needs to know that I don't play about my family."

"Okay, well you know where to find him," I replied.

Paul let us know he had something to take care of in his office, and went back inside the house. My sister and I went out to the garden and she gave me a pair of gloves to help her continue to pick her veggies. We then went into the house where I helped her wash her Kale greens, cucumbers, carrots, and strawberries for the salad she was including with her dinner.

My nieces ran into the kitchen when they saw me. Kristina was six and Cameron was eight.

"Hey big babies." I bent down hugging them both.

"Hey aunt Oba. We have new toys. Come see them." Kristina grabbed my hand and pulled me all the way upstairs. They showed me their new Barbie house and asked me to play. I stuck around with my family for a while.

Orion called a few times, but I was still thinking on that. I ate dinner and shortly after I left to go home.

Orion

Two days later

I have been calling Oba for the past two days. She hasn't been answering and it seemed like she was avoiding me. I could tell that she was sending me to voicemail every time because the rings were cut short. I don't know what's going on with her, but I'm about to find out.

I pulled up to her house seeing her car parked in the driveway. I got out and walked to her door ringing the doorbell and knocking at the same time. It took a minute, but she finally answered the door. I couldn't read her in this moment. Her face was blank of any expressions causing me to be confused.

My eyes moved down her body. She had on those little as boy shorts that showed her fat ass. Her breast looked succulent in the half shirt she had on. Her hair was wrapped with a bonnet on, but she still was fine as fuck.

"Hey," I greeted her.

"What are you doing here?"

"That's how you greet me after ignoring my calls for days?" I inquired. I took a step forward trying to enter her house, but she blocked me. I frowned asking, "Did I do something wrong? We were good just the other day.

She sighed as she stated, "You shouldn't be here."

"Fuck that. You are going to have to tell me something."

She looked away, tapping her foot before she sighed and turned her head back towards me.

"I have a lot of thinking to do. I got in trouble at work because Tommy sent an email to my bosses boss about you and I."

"What?"

She continued to explain the situation. I pushed out a sigh raking my hand down my face. This was some bullshit.

"You trying to cut me off for that?"

"Orion..."

"Nah." I forced my way inside before shutting and locking the door.

"You didn't do anything wrong, plus I am no longer a patient." I stepped closer to her and her chin fell to her chest. I gently placed my finger against her chin lifting it back up. I searched her eyes for her truth as I asked, "What do you want, because that's all that matters right now." I licked my lips wanting to feel hers against mine.

"I like you...a lot."

"Then what's the problem, baby?"

"You don't understand," she retorted.

"Well help me understand, Oba. I have an attraction to you that I've never had with any other woman. I can't let you go. Not for some bullshit. Tell me you don't want me." I pressed my lips against hers letting them linger. She didn't pull away therefore, I took it as a good sign. My hands moved down to her ass as I squeezed that big mutha fucka hard as hell. I was awarded with a sexy ass moan.

"I can't tell you that, because it wouldn't be true," she whispered.

I slid my tongue into her mouth as I lifted her from the floor. Her legs circled my waist as we passionately kissed. I walked her back to her bedroom and lay her on the bed. I pulled away and removed my shirt. I then reached forward and removed hers. Her breast sat lovely calling my name. I leaned down pulling her right nipple into my mouth. I sucked and tugged that shit while squeezing the other.

"Mmm," she let out as my hand moved between her legs. As soon as my finger slid up and down her slit I was ready to enter her.

"Shit, you wet as fuck. You going to let me get some of this pussy." I slid a finger into her pussy waiting on her answer.

"Please."

I hooked my fingers in her shorts and slowly pulled them down her legs while gazing into her eyes. I then removed the rest of my clothes. Her eyes moved to my hardened rod while licking her lips. Her hooded eyes moved to mine as she slid back onto the bed. I bent down pulling a condom out of my pocket, opened the gold wrapper and sheathed my dick. I got on the bed pushing her legs back lowering my head kissing each of her thighs. I made a trail to her pussy before licking up and down her folds before latching on to her clit.

"Oh shit," she hollered as she gushed. She must haven't had anyone eat her pussy in a minute because she instantly came. Her legs were quaking like hell as I moved up her body. I slid my tongue into her mouth at the same time that I entered her slippery pussy.

"Got damn, Oba." Her shit was snug. That last nigga couldn't have been hittin' it right. I slowly moved in and out of her with my eyes closed. When I opened them, hers were closed and I demanded through clinched teeth, "Look at me when I'm in this pussy."

Her eyes popped open as I pushed her legs all the way back to her ears, holding them down with my arms.

"Orion, ooo damn."

"That's right. This good ass pussy." I moved faster causing her ass to scream. Her shit was creaming. I wish I didn't have this barrier between us, but it was our first time.

I let her legs down placing one over my shoulder. I thrust long and hard before having her turnover. Her ass was high in the air. I pulled her ass checks apart before thrusting into her hard from the back.

"Shit." She was throwing her ass back at me. I smacked her ass watching it to ripple. Her back was sweaty and I leaned down licking it. I grabbed her waist slamming into her pussy. She hollered my name and I grunted as I continued to assault her pussy.

"Fuuuck," I hollered as I pushed her down. I lay on top of her rolling my hips. Her body trembled and my stomach caved in.

"I'm about to nut baby. Give me one more." She moved her ass up and down as she yelled and her pussy got juicer. Right after I came hard. I moved my hips placing kisses against her back until I was empty. I gently pulled out and she turned over.

"That pussy good, baby."

She blushed as her arms circled my neck. She pecked my lips saying, "And this dick is good, and mine."

I smirked not having a problem with that at all. After being up in her pussy, I didn't want no other bitch. Oba was all I needed. I got up to flush the condom down the toilet. She followed me into the bathroom where we went another round in the shower before washing each other up. We got out, dried off and got in the bed butt naked.

I held her in my arms rubbing my hand up and down her back. We were tangled in the sheets with our own thoughts.

"Baby, from now on, you can't just cut me off. Communication is the key in any relationship," I told her.

Her eyes opened as she asked, "We're in a relationship?"

"Hell yea, after that shit, you can't get rid of my add. You are mine. Is that a problem?" I raised my eyebrow awaiting her answer.

She rolled over on top of me straddling my lap as she replied, "No problems over here. She showed off her beautiful smile. She leaned down sliding her tongue into my mouth.

My dick hardened again and Oba took notice. She smirked as she lifted up sliding down my shit causing a moan to escape from my lips. This shit was even better without a condom. I held onto her hips as she slid up and down my shit. We were both moaning and groaning like we've never had sex before.

When she turned around fucking me reverse cowgirl, I lost my damn mind. Yea, she wasn't going no damn where. And Tommy was going to have to see me for trying to disrupt her life.

Chapter 8

Keifon

I asked Jenday to accompany me to the club tonight. Bizo was performing to promote his new single, and she agreed. I was waiting on her to finish getting ready when her front door opened. A man appeared that looked a lot like Leah. She was the splitting image of him, so I knew it was their father. He didn't appear to be a man with a cocaine addiction at first glance, but he did have on dirty clothes that looked like he had them on for days.

He glared at me as he made his way into the living room. I was about to speak until he asked, "Who the fuck are you and what are you doing in my house." I scoffed at his words. From what Jenday told me, his ass was never here. He had some nerve having an attitude when he was the one not taking care of his responsibilities. I wasn't going to disrespect him though, he was still Jenday's father. Instead, I stood up holding my hand up introducing myself.

"Hey sir, I am Keifon, a friend of your daughter."

He narrowed his eyes at me not even attempting to shake my hand and asked,, "Which one?"

"Considering, Leah is too young for me, I would think common sense would kick in and you would know that I am here for Jenday."

He cocked his head to the side and asked, "Are you standing in my house with an attitude?"

"Daddy?" Leah walked into the living room. She walked right up to her father and asked, "Are you giving Keifon a hard time? Leave him alone, he is fine here."

Her father turned to Leah kissing the top of her head. He pulled away and turned back to Keifon, "How long you've been with my daughter?"

"Not long," I replied. He stepped closer to me staring.

"I may have an issue right now, but I will do anything for my daughters. If you hurt her in any way, you will have to deal with me."

Laughter was on the tip of my tongue. I swear it was taking all I had in me not to say something out of the way. I believe Jenday can take care of herself and Leah better than her could right now. So again, I just nodded my head. He finally lifted his hand for me to shake just as Jenday came from the back of the house.

"I'm Keith by the way." He finally introduced himself.

"Daddy, what are you doing?" Jenday asked.

"Apparently meeting your man for the first time."

"You aren't around long enough to be able to meet anyone." She rolled her eyes.

I saw the moment Keith's eyes flashed with sadness. I could tell that it doesn't bring him joy to be an addict, he obviously couldn't help it. I kind of felt bad that he has that monkey on his back. He slumped his shoulders before kissing her forehead then he walked away towards the back of the house.

"You ready?"

"Yea, come on."

"Leah, I will be back a little later. Make sure Dad gets a healthy meal."

"Okay, see y'all later, have fun," Leah replied.

I guided Jenday out of the door by her lower back. I got a good look at her as she walked to the car. She was wearing a brown dress that stopped mid thigh. It meshed well with her skin tone. Her feet were covered in a pair of gold stilettos making her ass sit up. That thang was plump too.

"Damn you look good in that dress," I stated as I opened the car door for her. I didn't let her sit down immediately. I pulled her close pecking her lips a few times and squeezing that ass. I pulled away and then she was able to sit down in the seat. I got in on my side and pulled off.

The line was around the building of, *Groovy Nights*. I parked in my designated parking space by the door before getting out rounding the car and opening Jenday's door. I held out my hand and she took hold of it. We walked by the people standing in line and I noticed Prissy. She rolled her eyes at us and I looked towards Jenday when I heard her chuckle. Placing my hand possessively against her back? I leaned in for a kiss. She allowed me too which made Prissy smack her lips. I wasn't worried about that damn girl at all.

"What up Keifon," said Leon. He was one of the security guards that works for my father.

"Ain't shit." We slapped hands before he lifted the rope allowing us to go inside. It was thick up in there already. I know half these mutha fuckas in line not even going to be able to get in.

Women were speaking left and right, and I guess Jenday was feeling some type of way because she reached for my hand and intertwined our fingers. She was going to have to realize that she doesn't have to do all that, though. I lifted our hands kissing the back of her fingers as we made our way to the door that led to the gambling spot.

Another security guard from my Dad's company, Seth, spoke to me before opening the door allowing us inside.

"It's nice in here. A while different vibe," Jenday stated.

"Hell yea, it is. Come on, you want a drink?"

"Yes."

I led her to the bar and we sat down as we gave our orders to Lucky. She handed me my usual, Crown Royal straight, and Jenday ordered some fruity shit. I then grabbed her hand and we made our way to the little section that was only for my people and me. We sat in this spot in order to be able to look out and view the people making sure nothing pops off. Anything can happen when you're dealing with money.

We were chillin' when Orion and Oba walked in. My brother seemed happy, and I was loving it. Oba must really be changing him. They went to the bar and then joined us when they had their drinks.

"What's good?" We slapped hands.

"Just enjoying myself. This is Jenday, Jenday this is my brother and his I'm assuming, woman, Oba."

"Shit, hell yea she mine." Orion chuckled causing Oba to blush and giggle.

Orion spoke and then Oba held out her hand to Jenday and she accepted it. Oba sat beside Jenday and they instantly clicked.

"I love your hair," Oba told her.

"Thank you. Your outfit is on point," Jenday complimented.

"We can go out front and vibe if y'all want," said Orion.

"Yea, that's cool."

"Okay." They both stated as they stood up. We made our way through the gambling spot and entered the club. We led them upstairs to sit in our section.

Thot Shit, by Meghan the Stallion came on and they both went wild. Oba can dance, but my mutha fuckin woman stole the show. She was twerking in front of me, bending down joggling her ass. I kept pulling her dress down not wanting anyone to see my goods. Yup, I was claiming all that shit as mine.

"Ayyyeeee." She raised her hands in the air. When the song was over, she fell into my lap.

"I see you having a good ass time."

"Hell yea, I am." She leaned in and we tongued each other down.

Something told me to look up and I saw Prissy standing downstairs glaring at us with her arms cross. I smirked pulling Jenday closer to me. I pulled back gazing into her eyes.

"You are so dope, baby. I don't plan on ever letting you go," I whispered in her ear.

"I don't either." She pecked me once more before letting me know that she wanted another drink. I stood to my feet asking Oba if she wanted another as well. She said that she did and let me know what she wanted before I headed downstairs to the bar.

"You really doing this hun?" Prissy inquired.

"Gone head now," I stated flatly over the music and kept walking.

"I find it funny how you are just going to cut me off after all this time. I didn't even do shit."

"I found a better woman." I walked from behind the counter since I was finished fixing the drinks. Prissy got in my face and mushed my head.

I turned slowly placing the drinks on the counter and jacked her up by the front of her shirt as I grit, "Keep your hands to your fucking self."

"Babe, is there a problem?" Jenday appeared out of nowhere. I didn't even see her ass coming.

"Nah, I was just letting her ass know that it was a done deal."

"Alright, well let her go." She placed her hand on my arm and I let Prissy go. Something about her touch relaxed me.

"You see how he did me. He is going to do you the same way."

"I doubt that because he knows I don't play that shit. Now run along and enjoy yourself. Find a man who actually wants you," Jenday stated.

"Come on girl, he's not worth it." Prissy's friend was pulling on her arm.

"You haven't heard the last of me." She turned and stomped away.

"You good?" I asked Jenday. She smiled.

"Always." I grabbed her drink handing it to her then lifted the other three before we made our way back upstairs.

We partied for a few more hours until the club closed. When we pulled off, Jenday asked, "Can we go to your house? My Dad is there with my sister, so she is good."

"You sure he is going to stay?"

"He always stays for a few days."

"Ahhight then." I made my way to my place while she called her sister letting her know that she would be home later this morning. Of course she had a lot of questions. Jenday had her hands full with her.

We pulled up to my townhome and I got out of the car before helping her out. She giggled almost falling while getting out of the car. She fell against me and I chuckled saying, "I see you feeling good."

"Yaaaaasssss," she sang.

We made our way up the steps that led to my door before I let us in. I was surprised when after I locked the door, she pushed me against the door attacking my lips. She pulled back long enough to pull her dress over her head. She stood in front of me in a thong and bra causing me to lick my lips.

I let her take the lead as her hands moved to my jeans unbuttoning them. She then pushed them and my briefs down my legs. She assisted me when I lifted my legs to take them off. My shirt was being pulled over my head next.

"You doing it like that, baby?" I asked her as I stood naked stroking my dick.

"Shut up," she demanded and I clamped my mouth shut. She was turning my ass on. She kneeled in front of me gripping my dick with her small, soft hands. She stroked it as she licked up and down before focusing on my mushroom shaped, thick head. She popped it out of her mouth gazing into my eyes. She then deep throated my shit causing me to moan.

"Got damn," I shouted gripping her locks as she bobbed her head. Baby was going in on my shit. She had my toes curling and stomach fluttering.

I tried to pull her up when I felt my nut rising, but she shook her head going harder.

"Give me that shit," she demanded before squeezing her jaws and humming. I instantly came with her doing that shit.

"Ahhhhh." I let out almost falling from my knees being weak.

"Get your ass up here!" I demanded.

She smiled as she rose to her feet. I yanked her to me and removed her bra. I then slid her panties down her legs. I stood up lifted her in my arms turning and placing her back against the door. I lifted her up in the air until her pussy was in front of my face. I ate the fuck out of that good pussy until she was creaming.

I let her down and carried her to me bedroom as we kissed. Our hands were all over each other. I gently placed her down on my king-sized bed. She slid up and I hovered over her.

"You sure about this?"

"Yes," she replied.

I reached in my nightstand retrieving a condom ripping the gold wrapper before placing it on. I leaned down sliding my tongue into her mouth. My hand was on her thigh pushing it back. I lifted my head admiring her face as I slid into heaven.

"Ooo." Her back arched off the bed, with her lips forming an O.

Her pussy was snug around my dick like I belonged there. I was in heaven right now. Shit, I didn't ever want this to end. I thrust in and out of her with precision. Her legs were spread as wide as they would go. I sat up on my knees holding on to her feet as I fucked her causing her to scream my name. I see why she wanted to come here instead; she was very vocal.

"Uhn hun. You love this dick don't you?"

"Ye…yeeees," she replied as I hit her deep. Pulling out, I tapped her thigh for her to turn around. I got off the bed pulling her to the edge. I smacked her ass cheeks before thrusting into her long and hard.

"Shiiiiit," she hollered. Sweat covered my face as I focused on making love to that pussy. I pulled out bending down and eating her tight ass. I turned her around letting her ass hang off the bed slightly. I then pushed her legs back to her ears and dropped my dick off in her.

"Yeeeessss Keifon. Fuck," she shouted boosting my confidence. We were now chest to chest as I moved my hips staying as deep as I could go. Her pussy gushed when I found her spot. Her body quaked as she experienced her third orgasm of the night. I pulled her left nipple my mouth as she screamed.

"I'm about to nut, baby. Come for me." I stood placing her legs against my shoulder, with my hands against the front of her thighs as I thrust as hard as I could. Each time she yelped. Her legs wouldn't stop shaking, and she came again with me right behind her. My body gave small trimmers until my balls were empty.

"Shit," I let out.

I scooted her up on the bed while our bodies were still connected. I lay on top of her careful not to smash her as we passionately kissed.

"I need more," she moaned.

As soon as she said that, I was hard again. I pulled out of her, yanking the condom off before swiftly entering her again.

"Got damn, I done fucked up."

Chapter 9

Tommy

A week later

I've been watching Oba with this nigga all day. This shit didn't sit right with me. Even after her job was threatened, she was still messing with him. I don't understand it. What does he have that I don't? She never handled me this way. They are showing public display's of affection and all. Oba and I have never done no shit like that. She acted like I was some secret or something. I'm starting to think that I was being used for sex or some shit.

I was sitting in this parking lot watching as they walked hand in hand into the mall. A tap at my window startled me. I jerked my head back, glaring into the eyes of Paul, her brother-in-law. I sighed before rolling down my window.

"Nah, get out the car?"

"For what?" I asked.

Instead of repeating himself, he yanked my door open and pulled me out of it. He threw me against the back door glaring at me. He punched me in my stomach causing me to lean over gripping my stomach with a cough.

"What the fuck, bro?" I slowly straightened my body still holding my stomach.

"Ain't no what. And I'm not your fucking bro. You know what you're doing. See, I've been having you followed ever since Oba told me you put your hands on her, and lost your damn mind. This is going to be my only warning. Stay the fuck away from her."

"Maaan, this don't even have shit to do with you. You fucking her too or something?"

He laughed before saying, "You must be out your damn mind. Let me explain something to you. I will go to war for the ones I care about. She is my wife's sister, therefore, she is included in that short list. You are acting psychotic because she doesn't want you. Move around." His eyes narrowed at me as he seethed.

I glared right back at him mad as hell. The audacity of him approaching me. I don't care what he says, it's something about this that ain't right. It's no way that he is going this hard for Oba for nothing.

"Yea ahhight." I smiled as I inched back to the drivers seat. I watched as he backed away then turned around all together. He fucked up trying to check me about my business.

I sat in the parking lot lifting my phone. I scrolled through my contacts finding Dola's number. He wanted to mess with me, I am going to mess with him too. I only have her number because Oba's phone went dead one day and she called me from Dola's phone. In this moment, I'm glad I saved it.

"Hello," she answered.

"Hey, Dola."

"Who is this?" She inquired.

"It's Tommy, don't hang up, I have some information for you."

"What the hell could you possibly have to tell me. You have some nerve after what your delusional ass did to my sister."

"You use the term, sister loosely. I just ran into your dear husband and found out some interesting information. Why do you think Paul is going so hard over her?" I laughed maniacally.

I was met with silence. Yea, I had her thinking. That's all I needed her to do. Put her mind in a place that she thinks what I was about to tell her was possible.

"Humor me," she replied.

"They are sleeping together."

"What!?"

Got 'em. I thought until she started laughing like hell.

"There is no way that is true. Get off my fucking phone and go see a therapist." She hung up. However, I smiled because I could imagine the thoughts flowing threw her head right now. Satisfied with what I just did. I crank up my car and pulled off.

Dola

That man is out of his fucking mind. He was playing with me, had to be. There was no way that Oba and Paul are sleeping together. It's just not possible. I swear when he said that shit, my heart hit my toes. In a way, I felt he was trying to cause trouble because I know how passionate Paul is with the ones he love. Especially our families. On the other hand, Tommy has my mind fucked up.

I know that I'm wrong by even wanting to ask. But I had to for my piece of mind. I called my sister asking her to come over. She stated that she would be here when she drops Orion off in fifteen minutes.

When I hang up the phone, Paul walked through the door. He had a smile on his face as he stomped over to me and attempted to kiss me. I turned my head letting his kiss fall on my cheek.

He stepped back and asked, "You good? Why you seem mad?"

"Sit down, Oba should be pulling up in a minute."

"What's going on baby?" He stood in front of me. My jaw clenched as I avoided his eyes. He lifted my chin but I yanked it away.

I grit my teeth repeating, "Sit down."

He had a confused look on his face but sat down saying, "You trippin'."

"Maybe, but we will see."

Ten minutes later, the doorbell rang and I stood to answer it. Oba smiled until she saw my expression. I walked away without giving her our usual hug when we saw each other. She walked into the living room obviously realizing that something was going on.

"Sit down, Oba."

She listened and I sat in the recliner away from them both. Not wanting to beat around the bush I asked, "Have y'all ever slept together?"

Both of them reared their heads back. Paul narrowed his eyes asking, "What the fuck, baby? You know damn well that shit isn't true."

"What would make you ask something like that?" Oba questioned. Her face showed hurt mixed with anger.

I sat silently as I studied them both before saying, "I received an interesting phone call."

"From whom?" Paul asked.

"Tommy."

Paul's stomach rumbled as laughed asking, "How did that nigga even call you?"

"Is it true?"

"No!" They both shouted.

"He must have kept her number when I called from her phone a long time ago. I can't believe you would believe that Dola. You are my sister, and I love you. Paul and I would never do anything like that to you." She began to cry.

"Dola, that nigga mad because I checked him. I had him followed and my people told me that he had been following her and Orion all day."

"What?" Oba frowned.

"Yea, I pulled up at the mall and watched as he was staring at y'all enter the mall. Baby, you know I would never hurt you. Oba, do you know where he lives?"

"Yes."

"Let's go," Paul demanded.

"Michael," he shouted upstairs then their son appeared at the top of the stairs.

"Yes sir."

"Watch your sisters, we will be back."

"Okay, Dad." He turned probably going back to his room.

The three of us loaded into Paul's Suburban, and twenty-two minutes later, we were pulling into Tommy's driveway. We got out of the car with Oba and I behind Paul as he rang the doorbell.

Tommy answered and when he saw us, he smiled saying, "Is someone in trouble?"

"Tommy, you are a fucking liar. Too bad it didn't work," said Oba.

"Am I?" He replied.

My husband must have had enough because he started beating his ass. It was so bad that Oba and I had to pull him back. Tommy was on the floor in his doorway with a bloody face. He licked the blood off his lips as he laughed.

"Stay the fuck away from my family or you won't get up next time."

"Fuck you, nigga. This ain't over."

"Come on Paul, his neighbors are looking." I pulled on his arm.

"Yea, you heard what I said."

We walked away to Tommy shouting about how he does what he wants and we have to see him. That statement didn't sit well with me. When we were in the car I started crying.

"I'm so sorry. I knew it wasn't true. I know y'all wouldn't hurt me."

"Sis, it's okay. I forgive you." I nodded my head as Paul pulled me into a hug.

"Hey, we are good. I don't like that you believed it and shit, but I love you and we will always work things out. Just don't let that shit happen again." He placed a kiss to my lips before guiding me into my car. I vowed to never believe bullshit again.

Chapter 10

Keifon

A month later

"Yo, your food always hit the damn spot," I said to Leah. Shit, she can cook just as good as her sister.

"Thank you, Keifon."

I have been over Jenday's house for the past two days. I loved being around her fine ass. Then that pussy was a plus. I can't get enough of that shit.

"What you getting into today?" Jenday asked me. I let her know that I wasn't really doing shit until I had to go to the gambling spot later. She was about to respond when her cell phone rang.

"Hello...."

"Yes, this is she." I listened as her facial expression changed from relaxed, to panicked. Her breathing picked up, and tears sprang to her eyes. I was on my feet that next second, kneeling in front of her.

"I'll be there in a minute." She hung up the phone, her head falling into her hands. Leah and I glanced at each other.

"What's wrong?" Leah asked.

She didn't answer my question, but she said, "We have to go Leah. Daddy is in the hospital. He overdosed." She looked into my eyes before standing up. She went to grab her keys but I couldn't let her drive like this.

"I got y'all. I'll drive."

"You don't have to do that."

I pulled her into my arms, pecking her lips and said, "I will always have your back. Now, let's go." She grabbed Leah's trembling hands and pulled her out the door with us. I know to them, it was like Déjà vu. I remember Jenday telling me that they received a phone call from the hospital when their mother passed away.

We pulled up to Novant downtown. After I parked my car, I pulled Jenday on one side of me, and Leah to the other. Both of them needed support and I will have both of them as long as they're in my life.

"Hey, someone called about my father, Keith Coley," Jenday spoke to the front desk attendant. The lady pressed a few keys on her computer searching his name.

"Here we are. He is still in the emergency room part of the hospital. I need your names to make you a pass, and then you can go on back to room number twelve." All three of them gave their names before making their way to the ER.

Keith had an IV in his right arm feeding him fluids. He looked weak as he lay in that bad. Leah stood beside her sister with her head against her body crying.

"Why does he keep doing this Jenday? Is he trying to kill himself or something?"

Jenday placed her arm around Jenday's shoulder and placed a kiss against her temple. I felt bad about their situation. No one wants to see their parents in bad shape. It was a sad situation.

"I don't think it's that, Leah. He is an addict. They don't always think straight." Jenday touched her father's arm rubbing it up and down. She moved her hand to his face and he began to stir.

I watched as his eyes peeled open and Leah threw herself onto him while crying.

"Daddy, I was so scared." She lay her head on his chest. Jenday also had tears streaming down her face. She always had something to say about her fathers situation. She hates that he let drugs take over him, but at the same time, I can tell she absolutely loves him and wants him to get help.

"I'm sorry, baby girl." His arm weakly lay against her back as he kissed the top of her head. He then turned to Jenday and said, "I'm so sorry." All three of them were crying. I decided at that point to have a talk with him. I would try anything to help the two of them not to be in so much pain.

"You have to stop this Daddy," Jenday stated. Keith looked towards me finally realizing that I was their.

"Hey, why don't you two give us a second. Go downstairs and get something to drink." I dug in my pocket handing Jenday twenty dollars.

"Okay, do you want anything?"

"Nah, I'm straight. Then again, you can bring me a sprite or something."

"Okay, come on Leah." She grabbed her sister's hand and they walked out of the door.

"What's up man?" I stepped up to his bed. He didn't say anything, he just glared at me. I raked my hand down my face and said, "Look, I really care about your daughter; both of them. I want them to be happy, but they can't do that with you going on like this. Leah, is always worried about you. She cries herself to sleep sometimes because she thinks you don't care about her. She feels that you are choosing drugs over them. You have to get help, man."

I waited for him to reply. More tears built up in his eyes as he asked, "She told you that?"

I nodded my head and replied, "Yes, we had a conversation the last time you left. Jenday was still asleep when I heard her crying. I joined her in the living room and that's when she really broke down."

The room was silent for a while. When he finally said something, he said, "I appreciate you being their for them as of late. Honestly, I tried. It's hard man. Every time I think about my late wife, I want more. I need help man, you have to help me. Get me into a rehab program or something. I have to beat this. I know it's too late to change how Jenday feels about me, but I can at least be there for Leah. I know they hate me."

"No, they don't hate you, Keith. They love you which is why they want you to get clean. They both lost their mother, they don't want to lose their father too. And no, it's not too late for Jenday. She still needs you in her life. We are going to get you into rehab, man. I will even pay for it. As soon as you get out of here tomorrow, I will have it set up. I will personally come get you and take you."

"You alright with me, Keifon. You alright with me. Thank you." He held out his hand and I reached for it shaking it.

Right then, Leah and Jenday walked back into the room along with a doctor.

"Hey, I'm Doctor Railey. How are you feeling, Mr. Coley?" The doctor asked.

"Oh, I've seen better days, but I'm alive."

"And incredibly lucky. I see you have people who love you. You should get and stay clean for them."

"I agree Doctor Railey." Keith had a saddened look on his face as he looked between Jenday and Leah.

"Just let me check your lungs, and heart and I'll be out of your way to let you spend time with your family."

Keith nodded his head as the Doctor did as he said. He let him know that his lungs and heart sounded good. Then he left out.

I sat and watched as Jenday and Leah spoke with their father sipping in sodas. I let them know that I was going to step out for a minute. I was going to go ahead and search for him a rehab facility to get Keith into.

Jenday

We've been here for over an hour with my Dad. He tried to get us to go home and get some rest, saying that he would be okay, but I wasn't having it. And I knew Leah wasn't either. Leah was sitting on the hospital bed, feeding my Dad like he was a child. It was something to see.

"Why she doing that man like that?" Keifon asked me.

"She's just worried." I turned sideways laying my head against him as he wrapped his arms around me and kissed the top of my head.

"Yea, I get it."

I stood and sat sideways on his lap. I gazed lovingly into his eyes. I saw a flicker of love behind them. That shit made my heart melt.

"You know, you didn't have to be here for us, but you did. You are a very caring man, and I..." I dropped my head then lifted it back up with tears forming in my eyes.

"What is it babe?" Keifon questioned in almost a whisper as he used his thumb to gently move it back and forth across my bottom lip.

"I love you."

He pulled back staring at me with a smile on his face. He gripped my chin pressing his lips against mine.

"I love you, too," he stated when he pulled away.

"Aww, y'all are so sweet. I have a brother now. It's about time sis," said Leah.

I had to laugh at her as I asked, "What you mean? And let's slow down. It's not like Keifon and I are getting married."

"Aye, let's keep this shit a hunnid. We are not getting married, yet. Shiiit, you stuck with me girl." He pecked my lips then tapped my shoulder for me to get up. He stood and stretched before walking to the bathroom that was inside of the room.

"I kind of like him, Jenday." My father stated causing me to smile.

"Oh yea?" I chuckled then continued to say, "I'm glad I stopped playing hard to get. You never know."

"That's my girl. Do you remember what I used to tell you when I was in my right mind?"

"Yes, you told me never to let a guy know you are interested right away, that they will respect you more for the chase. But not too much chase, because then they will get tired of you."

My Dad nodded his head as he responded with, "That's exactly how I got your mother. I chased her for almost two months. That woman gave me a run for my money." His voice was trembling and when he couldn't hold it in anymore, he burst into tears.

"I'm so sorry. I'm sorry girls. This is all my fault. Your mother is gone because of me. If I wouldn't have started this shit, she wouldn't have had to work so hard. It's okay if you blame me because I blame myself." He was crying like a newborn baby. I didn't know what to do. Leah hugged him and Keifon chose that moment to walk back into the room.

"Hey, what happened that fast?" He asked me and I just shook my head. Keifon kissed the top of my head and said, "Just go comfort him. I'll be right here. I'm not going anywhere." He promised.

"Thank you." I told him as I made my way over to my father and joined Leah hugging him."

Chapter 11

Orion
A few weeks later

"What are you getting into tonight?" Oba asked me.

"Since I can't be with you, I'm going to put in a little time at the club."

"Yea, I hate I'm at work tonight. It's been slow. Will I see you tomorrow?"

"I'll be here whenever you want me to be."

"Good to know. Well, my break is over. Call me when you are leaving the club. If I don't answer. I will call you back later."

"Alright, baby." We disconnected the call just as I pulled up to the club. I got out of my car and headed inside speaking to security and a few patrons along the way. The club was bumping already. I bobbed my head as I made my way to the bar.

"What's good, Lucky?"

"Busy as fuck. What you want?" She asked.

"Nah, you worry about the customers, I'll fix my own drink." I busied myself fixing me a shot of Vodka. I then made my way next door to the gambling spot.

I glanced around making sure that everything was okay. I saw Paul standing at the craps table. Ever since I found out that he was Oba's brother-in-law, we have become real cool.

"What's good, my nigga?"

"Chillin', winnin' this money. You know how it is." We slapped hands and he turned back around to roll the dice. This nigga was winning for real.

"Damn, bruh. You legit with this shit," I said.

Paul chuckled as he replied, "Hell yea. That's it for me though. I've been lucky so far." He gathered his winnings and walked away to the bar with me.

"How is my sis-in-law doing?"

"She's good. She'll always be good with me," I replied.

He nodded his head up and down. We both turned our heads when we heard, "Just let me in, I want to talk to that nigga."

"The fuck?" I started walking towards the door that separated the club from the gambling spot. When we approached the door, Harold, one of my Dad's security guards had the door cracked open and I saw, a guy standing there. It was obvious that whoever it was wasn't allowed back here because the haven't paid. For all they knew, this was where the offices were.

"Who the fuck is this nigga?" I asked Paul whose face was scrunched up when he opened the door to step out. I shut the door quickly so the person couldn't see inside.

"That's Oba's ex, Tommy."

"Oh word?" I smirked as I stepped in front of Harold.

"Is there a problem tonight, sir?" I put on my most professional voice.

Tommy looked me up and down before his eyes fell on mind. He sneered as he said, "Hell yea, it's a problem. You've been creeping with my lady, and you need to step out of the way."

This dude's eyes were glossy. He was either drunk as fuck or high. I took another step towards him saying, "You can't creep if the woman is single. Now, I advise you to get the fuck up out of my establishment before I put you out."

"Tommy, what the hell is your problem? Didn't I beat your ass and tell you to stay away from them? Do I need to teach your ass another lesson?" Paul had stepped up beside me.

"Ain't neither one of y'all niggas going to do shit to me." Tommy seethed.

"Aye my man, get out of here before I carry you out," Harold stated.

Tommy nodded his head up and down with a smirk on his face. He began backing up since he was clearly outnumbered.

"I got you my nigga. Oba is simply confused and mad at me right now. She'll be back."

"I highly doubt that since she's in my bed every got damn night."

That wiped the smirk off Tommy's face as he tried to get to me. Harold stepped in front of me pushing him back causing him to stumble backwards.

"Get the fuck out of here!" Harold yelled. Tommy glanced around noticing he had an audience. He then glared at the three of us and turned around leaving the club.

"That nigga is off his rocker," said Paul.

"Hell yea he is. Anyway, I need a drink." Me and Paul walked over to the bar. After our drink, I made sure everyone was out of the gambling spot and then Paul and I made out way outside of the club. We weren't out there but a few seconds when Tommy appeared out of nowhere.

"What's all that shit you were talking? Talk that shit now, nigga." I turned around seeing Tommy holding a gun. I smirked at his weak ass. He was really doing all of this because Oba no longer wanted him. He may as well get over that shit. People started scrambling to their cars to get out of the way.

"Bruh, you see this shit," I asked Paul.

"Yea, he out of his fucking mind." He chuckled.

"What you think Oba going to do if you shoot me?"

"She will forget about your ass and come back to me."

I laughed from deep in my soul. This guy was crazy as fuck.

"Oh, you laughing. See how you feel with this."

I hurriedly ducked out of the way pushing Paul to the ground just as Tommy let off a shot. In return, Harold shot him twice and he fell to the ground as he hollered out in pain. The people outside screamed as I heard someone

Screams could be heard around me. I hated this happened at my spot, but it couldn't be avoided. I stood making my way over to Tommy. He was on the ground bleeding from his abdomen. I held a smirk as I kneeled down whispering, "If you survive, and you come back at me, you won't survive next time, and the next bullet will come from my gun."

"Fu…fuck you," he said with bloody teeth.

Sirens blared in the distance. I stood up walking to Harold. He was panicking. I had to calm him down by saying, "You good Harold. You did your job. The security tape will show that. He tried to rob us is the story."

"Ahhight." Just as we finished talking, both the ambulance and police rolled into the parking lot. Everything moved quickly from there. The paramedics began working on Tommy, while I spoke to the police about what happened.

"This is your place of business?" The officer asked.

"Yes sir it is."

"Alright, explain to me what happened."

I ran down the story of Tommy attempting to rob us and how Harold shot him once he shot at us. Paul was agreeing with me adding his two cents in.

"If you need it, I can pull up the security app on my phone. It will show you the whole thing."

He told me to go ahead and I did it. The tape doesn't have the sound. But from looking at it, it looks like I was trying to talk him down. Then it shows him shooting at us while Harold shot him.

The officer agreed that it was self defense, all he needed to do was make sure that Harold had a license to carry. He looked the information up in his police cruiser and saw that he did indeed have a license to carry. Which I knew he did, it was a requirement that my father had.

The officer didn't see a need to bring any charges against him. However, the officer did say that if Tommy makes it, he will be under arrest for attempted robbery, attempted murder, and possibly having a gun with no permit if that's the case.

"I appreciate that, sir." I shook the officers hand, and then he then left with his partner right behind him.

"Alright, lets get out of here." We all then left considering this incident had vacated the club.

Oba

"We have a gunshot victim coming in. Two to the abdomen." One of the emergency department attendants shouted as the ambulance was unloading the victim. I wasn't even supposed to be working tonight, but someone asked if I could switch with them this week.

I noticed the police walking in before the paramedics wheeled in the victim. I was pulling on a pair of latex gloves when I noticed that the victim was Tommy.

"What the..." I whispered. Not because I gave a damn, but because I wanted to know what happened. He probably got his ass into some shit like he was some type of G, which he wasn't.

"Bay four." I snapped out of my daze.

He was rolled into the bay as he groaned and moaned. I began searching his body to see if the bullets were still in him or if they went straight through. He hadn't noticed that it was me standing there, but when his head slowly rolled to the side and saw me, he started panicking.

"It's yo...your...fa...fault."

I frowned not knowing what the hell he was talking about. I played my position being as professional as possible.

"Sir, please. Calm down so we can help you."

Brittany rushed over to help me along with a resident. She asked, "What do we have...oh..." Her eyes widened as she looked at me. I subtly shook my head and we got to work. A few minutes later, Dr. Brasher decided that he needed surgery right away. He asked that we take him to operating room one immediately. We got ready to transport him and was on our way.

Once we were on the elevator, I asked, "What happened to you, Tommy?"

"Your boyfriend."

"What? Well what did you do?"

Tommy said nothing. He was weak from blood loss. His eyes opened and closed as Brittany said, "You know he did something. I spoke to the police briefly and he said that Tommy attempted to rob two men at a club."

"Oh my God, what Club?"

"Uhm, *Groovy Nights*."

"That's Orion's club. I need to check on him. What the fuck." I was panicking not knowing what happened. I needed to know that Orion was okay.

"Girl, he has to be okay. If he weren't, he would be in this hospital too."

She had a point there, so I calmed down. We got Tommy situated in the Operating room. I was about to walk away when he grabbed my arm. He motioned for me to lean down and said, "This isn't over."

I pulled back and smiled then whispered in his ear, "Whatever you did, you deserved it. Stay the fuck away from me and my man, before next time, you not make it." His eyes then rolled into the back of his head as he passed out and Dr. Brasher got to work. I walked off letting Brittany be the nurse for this surgery. I had no interest in if he lived or died.

As I headed back to the ED. I pulled my phone out of my scrubs pocket and dialed Orion's number. He didn't answer which had my thoughts running all over the place again.

I stepped off the elevator and the first person I saw was Orion. I rushed over to him throwing my arms around his body. He chuckled as he wrapped his arms around me.

"What are you doing here. The police are here." I was worried that he was going to get arrested. He didn't say anything, so I continued with, "I was so worried. Tommy is here. Only reason I know what happened was because the officer told Brittany."

Orion glanced around as he pulled away asking, "Can you take a fifteen-minute break or something?"

It wasn't that busy tonight, so I asked for him to give me a minute and walked off to get permission from the charge nurse to take a brief break. I was back in front of him in two minutes pulling him towards the automatics door that led outside.

"What happened, why did you shoot him?" I asked. By the frown on Orion's face, I could tell that that is not what happened at all.

"Who told you that shit?" He rested his body against the brick of the building and pulled me between his legs.

"Tommy said, *your boyfriend did it.*"

Orion chuckled as he lifted his Charlotte Hornets hat and turned it backwards before placing it back on his head.

"Nah, that nigga came in the club trippin'. He was looking for me and shit. Paul was there too. I cursed his ass out and Paul and I went about our night. So, when we were leaving, Tommy appeared and pulled a gun on us…"

"Oh my God. What the fuck?" I expressed.

"Yea, he was talking all this shit about how if I wasn't alive, you would come back to him."

I jerked my head back with my face scrunched up. I shook my head saying, "Tommy is delusional if he thought I would take him back. I don't care if we don't work out, it still wouldn't be his lame, square ass. I need a little excitement on my life." I leaned in pecking Orion's lips.

"Oh yea?" He asked rubbing on my back.

"Hell yea," I admitted as he leaned closer sliding his tongue into my mouth.

"Mmm," I let out. His hands moved to my ass squeezing it tightly.

He pulled away saying, "Girl, you better stop all that moaning before I take you to my car."

"If only I had time."

"Oh word, you down with that?" I nodded my head and he told me, "Good to know. So next time I come up here on your lunch break to get some pussy, I don't want you trippin'."

"I won't." I pecked his lips again.

We were silent for a minute then he admitted, "I didn't shoot him by the way. He let off some shots and Paul and I ducked down. My security shot him. I see you were worried when I first walked in with the police being there. They saw the tape. No charges against Harold, but Tommy will be in police custody when he gets out of surgery or whatever."

"Thank God. Good for his ass." I checked the time on my watch and said, "It's time for me to get back in there. I'm coming to you when I get off. That's cool?"

"You don't even have to ask." We then kissed once more before I walked away to get back to work.

Tommy Strum

I woke up groggily groaning from the pain coursing through my body. It felt like I was hit by a dump truck. I can't believe I did that shit, but the only thing I regret is not shooting that nigga. At least he would be dead or laying in the same hospital with me.

I have no idea how much time had passed, but judging by the brightness of the sun shining through the window, it was now daylight. I breathed heavily as I tried to lift my arm to my stomach. I looked down seeing that I was cuffed to the bed. *Damn.* I pulled my arm a few times like I was going to get lose or something. I fucked up, and I was going to jail. Maybe if I play my cards right, they won't lock me up. I have to think of something. I'm not built for jail.

I turned my head as the door opened. Oba walked in and I smiled until she said, "Shit, you made it." She said it like she was disappointed and was hoping that I died.

I scoffed as I replied, "You don't sound too happy about it." I shook my head and continued with, "You wrong as hell, Oba," I weakly stated.

She cocked her head to the side and asked, "How?"

"I heard everything you and that other bitch said in the elevator. You were more worried about him than me, and I'm the one shot the fuck up!" My last words were higher and I yelled when I tried to sit up because I felt every inch of pain. This shit hurts like a bitch. Oba is the damn nurse and didn't even try to help me, her ass laughed.

"This is funny to you?"

"Hell yea, especially since you tried to lie and say my man shot you."

"Don't call him that shit." I hollered.

"What, my man?" She shrugged and continued with, "What else would I call him when he is indeed, my man." She held a sly smirk on her face.

"He is temporary." I looked away from her and once I was looking at her, the look on her face wasn't a happy one.

She lifted my chart and looked down at it. She searched the documents and I saw the exact moment that she saw that I was on Zeldox. That was something that I never wanted anyone to know. Women always looked at me differently when they found out. She glanced at me placing the chart down.

"I'm going to go, Tommy. Feel better, okay?" She left quick as hell.

I guess my secret was out now. I am Bipolar. It gets bad when I don't take my meds. I'm sure that's why I made the stupid decision to try and shoot Orion, and Paul in a parking lot full of people. I had been missing my medication here and there for the past few weeks. Sometimes when I take those pills, it makes me feel like I'm not normal. My medication is supposed to help, but it doesn't. It's just that when Oba left me, I wasn't interested in being better.

I don't understand what it is about me that has women wanting to leave me. I'm Bipolar, not crazy. Sure, I put my hands on her, but it wasn't that bad.

"Hello Mr. Jones. Welcome back. I am Doctor Bresher, How are you feeling?"

"I'm not sure. I guess I'm alive is what counts."

The Doctor nodded his head. He looked over a few things before letting me know that I would have to stay in the hospital a few days. He then told me that the police were right outside the door to speak with me. I sighed as the Officer stepped inside. I was fucked unless they bought this act about me not being on my meds. Yea, that's what I'm going to do; act like I've lost my mind.

"Mr. Jones, I am detective Pearson. You do know why you are here in cuff right?"

I scrunched my face like I didn't understand what he was saying. I narrowed my eyes at him saying, "No, I don't."

Officer Pearson smiled while saying, "You do remember walking into a club causing a ruckus. You attempted to rob some men in the parking lot and was shot by security."

At the mention of a robbery, I was confused. That's not what happened at all, but obviously, that's how that nigga played it. *Smart man.*

"Someone shot me? I hope they are being arrested." I did my best to look confused.

Officer Pearson cocked his head to the side and asked, "Sir, are you feeling okay?"

I smiled while saying, "I'll be fine if I get out of these cuffs." I began yanking on the cuffs and thrashing around in bed.

"Let me out of here. Please. Let me out." I hollered.

"Unfortunately, Mr. Jones, that can not happen. Calm down."

I continued to move around. He made his way to the door and asked for help. A few nurses rushed in and tried to hold me down including Oba. I smiled subtly at her as she looked on wide eyed. The next thing I knew, a needle was inserted int my arm and whatever was in that needle calmed me instantly.

"Mr. Jones, you are charged with; attempted robbery, attempted murder, and possession of an unregistered firearm. You have the right to remain silent. Anything you say can and will be used…"

The officer was reading me my charges, and rights. But before he could finish, I had dosed off.

Chapter 12

Jenday

My father was now out of the hospital. Keifon did as he said he would and found him an inpatient rehab center, Brite life recovery. Me, Leah, Keifon and my father arrived at the facility and we all helped him get settled in his room. I was impressed with the facility. It was clean and the staff was amazingly nice.

Keifon placed his suitcase on the table that was against the wall, and my sister unpacked it putting the few items that he had into drawers. He wasn't allowed much. Only clothes, and he was allowed a few books to help him pass the time. He will not be able to have his cellphone or any other electronics. The place had a communal area that had computers, and even phones that people could use during certain times of the day.

"Mr. Coley, you can visit with your family for a little while, but you have to be ready for dinner in the cafeteria by six o'clock." Rebecca, the lady from the front desk stated.

"Thank you." My Dad said as he sat on the bed. I walked over to him sitting down. I bumped his shoulder as I smiled at him. My Dad is so handsome. I miss his joyful personality. Hopefully, after this, he will stay clean and we can begin to heal and become a family again.

"I'm proud of you Dad."

"Me too," Leah added sitting on the other side of him. He grabbed a hold of both of our hands lifting each of them one at a time to kiss them.

"That means the world to me, girls. I promise, that once I get through this shit, you don't have to worry about me at all." He then turned towards me and said, "I know that you are a grown woman now, and you don't need me…"

"I've always needed you Dad, and I always will. I do not care how old I get." I leaned over pecking his cheek before laying my head on his shoulder. The whole time my sister and I were speaking with my Dad, Keifon was right outside of the door conversing with Rebecca. A few minutes later, he came inside the room while glancing at his watch.

"Alright y'all, it's five-thirty, we have to get up out of here."

Leah started crying as she held on to our Dad. He lifted her chin with his finger and said, "Hey hey, I am going to be okay now. I will be out of here in no time." He stood pulling Leah with him, and then pulling me up as well and the three of us stood there hugging.

When I pulled back, I noticed my Dad wiping his tears. It was an amazing moment.

"We'll see you in a month, Dad."

"Okay sweetie. Keifon, take care of my girls while I'm gone."

"I got you." Keifon replied as he and Keith slapped hands engaging in a bro hug. After sharing another hug with us, the three of us left out.

Inside the car, I had a saddened look on my face. Keifon reached over placing his hand on my thigh rubbing it gently. He then looked back at Leah.

"He's going to be good. When he gets out of here, he will be as good as new. It will be a long road ahead, but I have faith that he will beat this. I can tell how much he loves y'all."

"I hope so," Leah whispered.

"I'm sure of it. Until then, I got y'all for whatever y'all need." The car fell silent as Keifon pulled out of the parking lot. He stopped at Chick-fil-A to get Leah, and I some food before heading back to my house.

Later that night, we were all watching a movie on Prime. It was a romantic comedy. Leah fell asleep by the time the movie was over. Keifon covered her with a blanket, and then we headed to my bedroom. I closed and locked the door before removing my clothes.

"I'm about to take a shower."

"Shit, me too." Keifon chuckled while removing his clothes. We washed each other up, before stepping out, drying off and getting in the bed. Keifon pulled me close engulfing me in his arms as I lay my head against his chest.

"Thank you," I told him.

"For what, baby?" He rubbed his hand up and down my side.

"For handling things for me. I appreciate it, because if it weren't for you, my Dad would probably be back in the streets."

Keifon flipped me on my back settling between my legs. He leaned down pecking my lips a few times before saying, "You don't have to thank me for that. Like I said before, I am here for the both of you. If you're happy, that makes me happy."

I smiled as tears sat at the rim of my eyes. Keifon sincerely cared about my sister and I, and I don't think he realized how that makes me love him even more.

I felt his dick hardening between my legs. My body heated up as I reached between us lining his dick up with my pussy. He kissed my tears away as he worked his way inside of me.

"Mmm." We simultaneously moaned in satisfaction. We kissed hungrily as he thrust his hips.

"Shit woman." He let out as he lifted my right leg over his shoulder without missing a beat. My body shivered as my hands moved to his ass pulling him in deeper. He was now hitting my spot over and over again. He stayed deep as he moved his hips in a circle causing my pussy to get wetter. I felt my juices running down the crack of my ass as I praised him with my words, and moans over and over again.

Keifon grunted as he repeated my name, then told me, "I love you."

"I lo…love you, too." He pulled out of me flipping me onto my stomach. I was in the doggy style position, but he pressed down on my back causing me to lay flat. Using his knee to open my legs further, he then entered me in one thrust. He beat my pussy up so good that I had to put my face in the pillow so I wouldn't wake Leah up.

Keifon pulled out and licked me from my ass crack, to my pussy.

"Damn." I let out moving my hips back and forth. He latched onto my pussy sucking until my body trembled and I released.

"Ooo, make love to me, baby."

He raised up pulling my ass cheeks apart before entering me slowly. His thickness felt so good that I wanted to cry. I glanced back watching him, watch himself making love to me. When he caught me looking, he leaned down crashing his lips into mine. I pushed my ass back against him as he was hovered over me. I then felt the weight of his body against mine. I felt his breath against my ear as his tongue swirled around the inside of it. He thrust deep causing me to yelp. Pulling out, Keifon flipped me back over onto my back. Keifon and I made love all night long until I couldn't take it anymore.

******

The next day

Leah and I spent quality time together by cooking dinner. We laughed having a great time. I wanted to take Leah's mind off of the situation with our father, and it seemed to help. Once we were finished cooking, we sat at the table and ate our Shrimp, Crab legs, Mac and cheese, and a salad. Afterwards, Keifon called letting me know that he had some things to handle and would see me at, Exquisite, later because I had a set tonight.

Leah and I sat on the couch watching TV. I checked the time seeing that it was already nine o'clock and I had to get ready.

"You going to be good while I'm gone?"

"Yes, I have to finish reading this book for school. I will be glad when the year passes and I can start twelfth grade."

"Have you been looking into any colleges?" I asked her. Leah was smart as hell; she took the Pre-SAT's this summer and made a 1400. I was extremely proud of her.

"Yes, I think I want to stay in Charlotte. I want to go to Johnson C Smith, but I filled out an application for UNCC, UNCG, and Winston Salem too. I just want to stay close to you and Dad."

"Whatever you decide, you know I support you." I smiled at her and she threw her body against mine as we hugged. I pulled away saying, "Alright, I am about to go shower and get ready to leave."

"Okay," she replied and I stood from the couch heading to my bedroom. I took a shower, moisturized my body, and threw on a pair of tights, and a t-shirt. I packed my outfit that I was performing in. I walked back to the front seeing Leah on the couch reading.

"I'll see you later, Leah." I kissed her forehead.

"Okay. Love you."

"Love you, too."

******

"Hey, Jenday." Walt spoke to me as I entered the club through the employee entrance.

"Hey Walt, I see the parking lot is full."

"Hell yea, you know how it is when you're working."

I smiled at him as I continued to the dressing room to get ready. I had to hit the stage in thirty minutes. I pulled my outfit out which consisted of a hot pink thong, and a bustier with rhinestones on it. After getting dressed, I slipped my hot pink stilettos on my feet. I rubbed body butter with glitter on my body and I was good to go.

I stood at the stage behind the curtain waiting to be announced.

"Good luck girl. Do your damn thing," Goldie said.

"Thanks girl." Right then, the DJ announced my name. So Anxious by Genuine blasted through he speakers. The bass hit my body as I sauntered out on stage. The lights were dim and the spotlight shinned bright on me once my body moved to the beat.

I'm so anxious so meet me at eleven-thirty
I love the way you're talkin' dirty said I'm
So anxious girl could you quit this stallin'
You know I'm a sexaholic said I'm…So anxious.

I dropped down to the ground rolling my hips. I stood with my ass towards the crowd before slowly walking to the poll. I climbed up it and hung upside down using my arms to allow my legs to swing loosely in the air. I then dropped down into a split. I continued my set until the song was over. Of course I got a standing ovation. I smiled looking out at all the money on the stage. I walked off as my money as gathered. I stood there waiting for it and then grabbed the bag.

I went to the dressing room and put my tights and t-shirt back on. With my bookbag on my back I walked out front. I was looking for Keifon the whole time, but he never came. He must have been tied up at his club or something. I wondered why he didn't call and tell me he wasn't coming. I picked that song specifically for him.

As I walked through the crowd headed towards the door, Prissy appeared in my face with two of her friends.

"I can't believe Keifon left me for a stripper bitch."

I jerked my head back glaring at her through narrowed eyes as her two little friends laughed. People around us heard what she said and focused on us. I smirked as I replied, "Did you see how my body moves? Bitch, that's why." I chuckled.

Prissy frowned saying, "And you proud of that shit?"

I shrugged, this girl just does not realize how irrelevant she was. She was standing in my face like she mattered. My smile stretched even more as I replied, "It's a fact. I make more money here than you can get from the niggas you be fucking to get money. I don't have to fuck. I have a talent and I use that shit to take care of my family. So call me a hoe or whatever you want, because this hoe securing the bag on her own. Now excuse me, I need to get a drink before I go to my mans house and put this pussy on his mouth."

"Ooooo."

"She told her ass."

"Give it up boo, he don't want you." Was what I heard from the crowd. I stepped around her to the bar and ordered my drink. The look on her face gave me satisfaction because I knew for a fact that he had never ate her pussy, nor has she ever been to the real place that he rest his head. I ordered a Cîroc and cranberry waiting for Keifon to call me. If he didn't call before I finished my drink, I was going to go home and get in bed.

I nursed my drink for twenty minutes. I figured Keifon was busy, so I prepared myself to leave. I spoke to a few people headed towards the door. The cool air hit me on the face as I made my way to my car. I was almost there when I felt someone yank my book bag from my back.

"Bitch, give me this shit." I heard Prissy. I had a good grip on my book bag because no one was going to take my shit. Her friends joined in and we struggled for the bag.

"Bitch, you must be out your fucking mind." I shouted feeling fist come at me from three different directions. I was pushed to the ground and the bag was taken from my hand. Where the fuck was security. I fumbled with my keyring and sprayed mace in Prissy's face.

"Ahh." She screamed as she dropped the bag on the ground. I stood up grabbing it.

"Who else want some?" I held the mace up and her friends backed up holding their eyes. Some of the burning liquid got in their eyes as well.

"What the fuck is going on?" I heard Keifon's voice, but kept my focus on the three women in front of me as they rubbed their eyes making shit worse.

"These bitches tried to take my money. Baby, if you can't control this bitch, and her minions, I'm going to handle the shit myself. I'm not for the drama and you know that." I dropped my arm seeing as if they couldn't come at her anymore.

"I don't play about three things; my family, my money, and you." I finally turned towards him.

"I got you baby." He pulled me into a hug pecking my lips. He then pulled away and walked towards Letty. He bent down and she glared up at him barely able to open her eyes.

"Have you lost your mind?"

"Fuck you Keifon," she hollered.

"Hey, what's going on here?" Security finally rushed over.

"Where the fuck were you at when these women were attacking my woman?" Keifon got in the man's face.

The security guard frowned saying, "My bad, I didn't know."

"That's obvious nigga. Now what's going to happen is these hoes going to get banned, or I'm going to have you replaced."

"Nigga please. You don't have the authority." He smirked.

"Lets see about that." Keifon pulled out his phone and made a call.

"Yo Pops. You know that club Exquisite?"

I couldn't hear what his Dad was saying, only his side.

"Yea, that's it. They may need your services. Call the owner tomorrow about getting someone from your team…"

"Alright, I'll be over that way tomorrow. I have someone I want you to meet..." He listened to his Dad, and then disconnected the call with a satisfied smirk.

"Come on, man. That's not even called for. I need my job."

"Well then, you know what you have to do. Come on, Jenday." He grabbed my hand and he walked me the rest of my way to my car. He opened the door and removed my book bag throwing it on the passengers seat. He then turned me around and pulled me close.

"I'm sorry, baby. She is not going to bother you again. If she does, she will regret it." We turned towards Letty and her friends when we heard them arguing with the security guard. I knew he was going to make the right decision not wanting to lose his job.

"That bitch is crazy. I know why she like that, though." I smiled.

"What's that baby?"

"She miss that dick. It's mine now, though." I grabbed his dick squeezing it.

"You better stop that before you start something." He raised his eyebrow.

"How you know I'm not trying to start something?" I licked my lips sliding my hand down his pants. He closed his eyes as he grunted.

"Get in your car, and lets hurry to your house, girl."

I smirked as I got in my car ready for whatever. He headed to his car and we left the parking lot.

Oba

Tommy was still in the hospital. I tried my best not to go in his room, but when there was no one else available, I had no choice but too. I really think he was pressing the call button on purpose until I came in.

I took a deep breath before entering the room with a smile plastered on my face. When he saw it, he smiled back. He must have thought I was reconsidering or something he seemed a little to happy to see me.

"Do you see it now?"

My smile turned into a frown as I asked, "See what?"

"How much I love you. I got shot because I want you back. That nigga gotta to go?"

"What? No, you got shot because you were being stupid. That has nothing to do with your so-called love for me. And Orion isn't going anywhere. You see how that went right?"

Tommy moved his eyes from my face, to my perky breast, and thick thighs. His eyes misted over as he admitted, "I fucked up baby, please take me back. I'm sorry, please!" He wiped at his eyes. I couldn't believe this grown as man was laying here crying.

"I'm sorry for being to possessive, and putting my hands on you. Only thing I'm not sorry for is trying to kill that nigga. He ain't for you, Oba. Can't you see that? I think everyone deserves a second chance. Plus, you lied to me. You told me, that you weren't ready for a relationship and now you are in a whole relationship with another man!" He hollered the last part, and grunted from the pain that seared through his body from him trying to quickly sit up. He was really sitting here acting like a big ass baby. I shook my head as I chuckled. This man looked foolish right now.

"Tommy, sometimes, people are only meant to be in your life for a season. You were my season. What can I say, the dick was good." I shrugged then continued to say, "But if I'm being honest, you are not my type."

"But why not? Did I not treat you right? Did we not have fun? What is it?"

I pushed out a sigh and replied, "We had fun in the bedroom. You barely took me on dates nor did you romance me. Orion is all of that for me. When I think of him, my heart flutters. I'm sorry Tommy, but there is no hope for us. And there is no point of this conversation. I don't hate you, and I hope that when you get out of prison, you find a woman that wants to be with you as much as you want to be with her."

Tommy glared at me for a few moments, wiping the tears from his eyes. I saw the moment his eyes flickered from hurt, to anger.

"You know what, Oba. Fuck you. You ain't nothing but a hoe. You barely know that man. Fuck youuuuu!" He screamed at the top of his lungs.

The door swung open and Brittany rushed in, "Oba, are you okay? We can all hear him in the hallway."

"Fuck her. Get her out of here!"

"I'm okay Brittany. This grown ass man is just throwing a tantrum because I don't want him anymore." I giggled. This was the funniest shit.

"Fuck you, bitch!" He screamed again.

"Now Tommy, I need you to calm down or I will be forced to put your ass back to sleep." Brittany pulled a needle out of her pocket.

"Fuck you too! Don't you dare put that shit in me!" He was acting a damn fool. Brittany pushed the benzodiazepine into his IV. We stood there a few seconds watching him calm down.

"Come on girl." Brittany stated pulling me out of the room. A few nurses eyes were on me and I smiled letting them know that I was okay. I went about my day not even thinking about Tommy. My mind was on Orion who should be at my house when I got there. The rest of my shift went by easy since I was back on the morning shift. At exactly seven o'clock, I was out the door.

******

I pulled up to my house and smiled seeing Orion's Mercedes. I opened my garage and pulled inside as Orion got out of his car walking inside the garage with a vase in his hand before I pressed the button on my sun visor to close the garage door.

"Hey," I spoke to him as he handed me the flowers and then circled his arms around my waist.

"Thank you, I love them." I smelled the flowers.

"Ain't no thang. What's up, baby? You tired." He pecked my lips.

"I was when I was at work, but now I have a lot of energy. I just need to shower." He let me go and I unlocked my door then we entered my home. I dropped my keys and the flowers on the counter and headed to my bedroom with Orion following behind me.

"Tommy was my patient. He was tripping today. He tried to convince me to leave you. He said you were in the way, that's why he tried to kill you." I ran down the story as I removed my clothes.

"Maaan." Orion chuckled before saying, "I'm not worried about that nigga. You see how that worked out for him." He removed his shirt, then the rest of his clothes.

"That's the same thing I said. And you just knew you were going to get some pussy."

"I missed you. I need to feel that shit gripping my dick." He licked his lips. I giggled as I made my way into the bathroom turning on the shower. We stood there kissing and groping each other until the water was warm. He stepped in first and then helped me in.

We washed each other up before he pressed my back against the wall with his hands on my ass.

"Mmm." I moaned into his mouth as his hands moved to my folds. He strummed my pussy with his thick fingers.

"Baby, I need you now."

"Be patient." He lowered himself down, placing my foot on his shoulder. He sucked my clit sliding his finger inside me until my body shivered and I came.

He stood up saying, "We need the bed for the shit I want to do to your body." I said nothing as we washed up and then he carried me out of the shower, placing me on the floor and drying my body. After he dried his, he lifted me back up and carried me to the bed.

He lay me down gently, leaned down licking my pussy before hovering over my body. He pecked my lips a few times as he stretched my pussy wide open. We moaned as he pulled out and thrust back into me causing me to yelp. Orion steadied himself on his hands as he pounded into me with precision.

"Yes, baby." I placed my hands on his butt pulling him in deeper. He yanked himself out of me demanding, "Ass up." I hurriedly moved into position. He rammed his dick in me from the back causing my body to fall flat as I hollered, "Oh God." I moved to put my ass back in the air but he said, "Stay like that." He pushed my legs together and thrust in me so hard repeatedly that the bed shook. I pushed my ass back into him as he kissed all over my back.

I felt his weight lift off me. He pulled my upper body up so that my back was against his chest. He gripped my breast as he sucked on my neck, at the same time fucking me excruciatingly slow.

"Fuck, Oba. This pussy good as fuck."

"I love this dick. Ooooo." My eyes rolled into the back of my head. He used his fingers to apply pressure to my clit causing my whole body to tingle. I raised my arm placing it in the back of his head.

"Wet this dick up," he demanded.

Those words did something to my body, and I came instantly. He didn't stop, he thrust hard, pulling out slow. He repeated that over and over again. I began to see spots behind my eyes as he pulled out turned me back on my back and entered me.

"I need to see your face when you come again." He gazed into my eyes intently. Tears spilled from the corners of my eyes before they rolled into the back of my head.

"Come with me baby." And I did. My orgasm was so long that my vision blurred. My body went limp and I could hear him calling my name. The feeling was so damn magnetic. I felt like our souls were connected.

"Oba. Shit." Was the last thing I heard before my body elevated and I completely blacked out.

A few minutes later, my eyes fluttered open. Orion's dick was still inside me as he had a frantic look on his face.

"What happened?" He finally pulled out of me settling at my side.

"This good dick made you pass out."

I blushed covering my face. That shit has never happened before. His damn dick must be made of kryptonite.

"I did?" I asked.

"Hell yea you did." He chuckled as he pulled out of me laying at my side.

"Damn, that shit has never happened before," I replied.

"Damn is right." We both laughed as we settled in the bed. I was so damn tired that it took me no time to fall asleep.

Chapter 13

Jenday
Two months later

Today is a huge day for the family. My Dad is coming home today, and we planned a welcome home party for him. He ended up doing another thirty days to make sure he beat his sickness. I was so proud of my Dad for completing the program. We only talked to him about once a week, and a counselor also called weekly to give updates.

It was now fall and the perfect time for a cookout. A few months ago, Keifon, and Orion's mother had a dinner where she invited us over wanting to meet the women in her sons lives. They knew Oba from the hospital but wanted to get to know her better. Needless to say, her and her husband, Jahamal loved us. They thought that Oba, and I were great additions in their sons lives.

"Are you exited?" Iris asked Leah as we stood in the kitchen seasoning the meat to go on the grill, and the fish to be dropped in the deep fryer outside.

"Yes, I miss my Daddy more than you know. I just pray that he stays clean. He has already missed so much of my life." Leah smiled slightly.

"I am sure he will. I learned that most times, if someone agrees to go to rehab, it's because they want to. Him being rushed to the hospital probably scared him straight," Iris replied as she hugged Leah. This was her first time meeting my sister, and Leah liked her and vice versa.

"We don't have anything to worry about, sis. I know he can do this," I assured Leah. Our Dad was a sensitive subject for her. All these years, all she wanted was his attention and love.

"Is the meat ready to go on the grill, sweetheart?" Jahamal walked through the sliding doors and asked.

"Yes, you can take these steaks, and chicken. And the hotdogs, and hamburgers are also ready," Iris replied pointing to the pans of meat.

"Alright," He replied as he lifted one of the pans and carried them outside.

"Hey, Ma." Orion walked into the kitchen and kissed his mother on the temple.

"Hey baby," she replied.

Orion moved to Oba pulling her into his arms and asked, "You good?" He pulled back seemingly searching her eyes for confirmation. I loved their relationship.

"Yes. Now get out of here. Take these other pans to your Dad."

"Oh, you kicking me out the kitchen?" He raised his right eyebrow.

"Yes," Oba, Leah, Iris, and I stated simultaneously and then laughed.

"Oh I see how it is." Orion joked before pecking Oba's lips, then lifted the two pans going into the back yard with Jahamal.

An hour went by as we finished cooking the sides, and the men finished up the meat. Everyone was standing around conversing, waiting on Keifon to arrive with my Dad. I received a texted from my man stating that they were five minutes away.

"Okay y'all, they are about to pull up. My Dad has no idea that we planned this for him."

Leah jumped up and down excitedly. When we heard a car pull up, we all stood under the sign that said, *congratulations*.

Keifon walked through the door first, followed by my Dad.

"Congratulations," everyone shouted. My Dad's smile was bright, and he looked good. He had color back to his skin, and even looked like he gained an ample amount of muscles.

"Oh, y'all got me. I wasn't expecting all of this." His gaze fell to Leah and me as his eyes misted. Leah ran to him first jumping into his arms. He caught her holding onto her tight as they cried.

"I'm so happy Daddy." Leah held onto him. He motioned for me to come here and removed one of his hands from Leah putting it around my shoulder.

"I miss you girls so much." He held on a little longer. When he let go, Leah stayed attached to him.

"Dad, this is Oba, my friend. And this is Orion, her boyfriend, and Keifon's brother. And this is his mother, Iris, and Father, Jahamal."

My Dad stepped up and shook all of their hands saying, "It's nice to meet you all."

"Same here."

"Nice to meet you."

"It's a pleasure," they all replied.

"Alright y'all. It's a celebration. Let's say grace and eat." We all held hands, and Jahamal led us in grace. Afterwards, we headed to the kitchen and fixed our plates. We were having a good ass time. When we were finished eating, we sat in the living room conversing.

"You know Keith, I was in your same situation before. So I know you can do this. I am twenty years clean. Much like you, I had a scare, went to rehab and now I am married with a family, and I own my own security company. I would like to offer you a job if you want it." Jahamal told him.

"Really?" My Dad was surprised at the job offer.

"Yes, you deserve to have a chance for your family," Jahamal replied.

"Aww man. Thank you." Keith stood and he and Jahamal embraced each other.

"We can get your paperwork started Monday and get you going," said Jahamal when they pulled away.

The night went by well. My sister was happy. My Dad was happy, and I was happy. I couldn't wait to embark on this new journey with my sober Dad.

A few hours later, everyone started leaving. Keifon was going to leave saying we needed time alone with my Dad, but I convinced him to spend the night.

Leah and My Dad were sitting on the couch watching a movie. I smiled watching my Dad with his arm around her. My sister wasn't going to let him out of her sight if she didn't have to.

"Dad, I want to tell you again that I am extremely proud of you. I knew you could kick this. Now we just have to take it one day at a time." I leaned down hugging him.

"Thank you, Jenday. I am here to stay. We have a lot of time to make up, and I am willing to do just that. Sweetheart, I am so sorry that you didn't get to live out your dream by going to Julliard. That is one of the main things I regret besides losing your mother, and leaving the two of you to fiend for yourselves. I will never do that again. Y'all have my word." He looked towards Leah using his hand to gently rub her jaw, before turning towards me then continued with, "I love y'all so much." Tears cascaded down his cheeks.

"Oh Daddy. What matters is that you are here now." I smiled.

"Y'all have a good night. I will see y'all in the morning."

"Good night, sis."

"Good night, sweetheart."

I took one more look at my family before turning on my heels, and headed to my bedroom. I closed and locked my bedroom door hearing the shower water running. I removed my clothes, putting them in the hamper in the corner of my bathroom, and then pulled the shower curtain back joining Keifon.

As soon as I stepped in, Keifon was on me like white on rice. His hands gripped my ass pulling me close allowing me to feel his hardened dick. He crashed his lips into mine sliding his tongue into my mouth. He kissed me slow and passionately causing me to moan into his mouth. I pulled back after a few minutes and gazed into his eyes.

"All of these years, it has just been me and my sister. Then you came in like a thief in the night making my life ten times better. I appreciate that." My eyes misted from the emotions I was feeling because of this man. He used the pads of his fingers to thumb my tears away.

"You don't have to thank me for that. That's what your man is supposed to do." He pecked my lips.

"I know, but I want to thank you for being there for my sister and me. I love the way you helped us out with my father. You are a real one for that."

"You dealing with a real nigga now. And real niggas do real things."

This man was everything to me. I have never felt this way about any man I have ever come in contact with. I haven't had many, for the simple fact that my life revolved around raising my sister, and I am fine with that. God kept me single knowing that the man for me wasn't in my grasp yet. But now he is, and I love his ass with everything in me.

"Baby…" I whispered.

"What's up, Jenday?"

"Make love to me."

He stared intently in my eyes. It was like he could see all parts of me. Instead of doing what I asked all the way, he grabbed the rag, poured liquid soap on it, and washed my body from head to toe. In return, I washed him up. We then stood under the water rinsing off.

I lowered my body and sucked the hell out of his dick. I had to tell him to be quiet because he was moaning loudly. After he let a load off in my mouth, I cut the water off and we got out the shower, dried off and walked into the bedroom.

I lay back on the bed opening my legs as wide as I could. I squeezed my breast then moved one of my hands between my legs and toyed with my pussy.

"Mmm," I let out lowly arching my back.

"Shit, you look sexy as fuck. Dip them fingers in that glistening ass pussy."

I did as he asked. My eyes stayed on him. He was stroking himself while he watched me play in my pussy.

"Shit." He got on the bed knocking my hands out the way and sucked the hell out of my pussy. My body was still trembling as he climbed up my body and penetrated me. We both let out moans of satisfaction as he methodically moved in and out of my. He pushed my legs back holding them in place with his arms.

I licked my lips pulling his head down to get a taste of my pussy juices that were shining on his thick lips.

"Yes baby. Oh God, you feel so fucking good. Go deeper baby. I want to feel all my dick." My voice was low. He listened to me and granted me with deep strokes.

"I love you." He kissed my forehead.

"I love you so fucking much." He them kissed my nose. He said it once more before kissing my lips.

"I love you, too Keifon. I love you. Oooo." My mouth was wide open as I panted. My body quaked and the next think I know, I was squirting on his stomach.

"Shit, mutha fucka. You drowning this dick, baby."

"You made me do it. This dick is sooo good. Yes. Yes. Mmm."

Keifon made love to my soul just as I asked him to do. I didn't want this feeling to ever go away. I was stroking my pussy so good that it brought tears to my eyes. He kissed every last one of them away as his movements became frantic letting me know that he was on the verge of an orgasm. I clinched my pussy muscles pulling that nut right up out of him. He lowered his head placing his mouth on top of mine to muffle my moans as we experienced an orgasm together.

Keifon

We lay in bed basking in the glory of our orgasm. I gently pulled out of her pussy and lay beside her. I kissed her shoulder as she panted catching her breath.

I thought about a few things about my life that she didn't know about. I was sure that Jenday was my one and didn't want to keep secrets from her. I let our breathing calm before I told her, "I have been keeping some things from you and I feel you need to know the truth."

Her body tensed as she turned her head towards me. She was probably thinking the worse, but she didn't have to worry about no other woman with me.

"Calm down, it's nothing like that."

"Well what is it?"

"Alright so, you know I own my club and gambling spot or what not..." she nodded her head.

"Well, that's not all I do for money. My brother and I deal with this guy. He is basically the head of a Mafia. Bizo is also in this. Well, you remember when my brother got shot?" She nodded her head and I sighed before continuing to say, "Well, we were asked to steal six cars for two-million-dollars. Orion was shot when the guy caught us taking his car."

"Keifon..." She sat straight up with a frown on her face.

"I know. We have one more car and we out. I have to go to Atlanta next weekend."

"Keifon, I don't like this. Oh my God. What if something happens to you. I don't know what I would do. What if someone notices you in the future."

I shook my head and replied, "Not going to happen. We wear mask. No one has ever seen our faces. But I promise baby, after this last car, that's it."

She nodded her head and laid back down. She rubbed her hand up and down my chest as she asked, "Can I come? I can go shopping while y'all handle business. And Oba can come so I won't be alone."

I thought about it for a second before agreeing. I wouldn't mind getting away with my woman for a few days. We lay in silence until we fell asleep.

Hours later, I woke up to the smell of something delicious. I reached over, but didn't feel Jenday next to me. I swung my legs over the bed and stood heading to the bathroom to handle my business. I then pulled on a pair of shorts and a t-shirt before walking through the house to the kitchen. As soon as Jenday saw me, she smiled.

"Good morning, y'all."

"Good morning," the three of them repeated. Jenday stood walking to the stove and fixed my plate while I sat down. She sat the plate of French Toast, eggs, and bacon, with a bowl of cheese grits in front of me. I licked my lips before digging in.

"Baby, I have to leave after I eat, but I will be back later."

She poked her lips out and replied, "Okay."

When we were done eating, Jenday and I went into her bedroom. I tongued her down before putting on my shoes and telling her that I would see her later. I went back up front saying my goodbye's to Leah, and Keith before leaving. The first thing I did was go home to shower and get dressed. Puma texted me last night and asked that I come to the shop today. I have no idea what he wanted. We only had one more car to get and we were done with him.

******

I pulled up to the shop parking my car. I walked to the door and after being searched I made my way to Puma's office.

"What's up, Keifon."

"Hey man, what is this meeting about?" I asked as I sat down.

"Out of the three of you, you are my favorite. I called this meeting to see if you were sure about quitting. You guys have the potential to make a lot more money. You three are the best, but I know you are the brains."

I raked my hand down my face. More money would be great, but I was good on that. I wasn't going to get greedy, that's how people get caught.

"Nah, I'm good with what we have."

"You sure?"

"I am," I replied.

Puma stared at me before smiling, "Very well. You know, I am surprised that you and Orion are as close as you are."

I frowned not knowing where he was going with this. However, I had a feeling that I wasn't going to like it.

"Why you say that?"

"Because of what his father did."

I jerked my head back and asked, "What you talking about, Puma?"

"You ever wonder what happened to your father?"

"I know what happened. He was in the streets and got killed."

Puma chuckled as he shook his head. My stomach dropped because I had a feeling what he was going to say, but I prayed he wasn't.

"Nah, Jahamal killed him."

"What?" I abruptly stood up glaring at him. This shit couldn't be true. My mother never told me this shit.

"How do you know that?"

"Jahamal used to work for me back in the day. He killed that nigga then got with your mother."

"Nah man." I was livid at this point.

"It's true. I wouldn't lie about nothing as serious as this."

"Why are you telling me this shit now?"

"Because, I figured you would want to know who you call your brother, and Pops."

I don't know his reasoning, but I was mad as hell. I stood there for a second before bolting towards the door. I never questioned my mother when she received that phone call and had to identify my fathers body. I remember that day because she came to pick me up from our neighbors house all distraught. When she sat me down, and told me, I cried. My father had a lot of flaws, but he treated me well. If this shit was true, that means my mother has lied to me all my life. Not to mention Jahamal…if he did this shit…man. I don't know what I would do. I drove around for a while clearing my head I had to calm down before I went to see this nigga. It was Sunday and I knew my mother, and Jahamal were home. I parked in the driveway and sat there for a minute. The more I sat there, my calm faded away. I was mad as fuck. I got out of the car all in my feelings. I stomped to the door and banged on it like I was the police or some shit.

My mother opened the door with a pleasant smile, however, when she saw the look on my face, that beautiful smile dropped. My chest heaved as she asked, "What's wrong?"

I didn't say anything to her. I couldn't. I didn't want to disrespect my mother. But when Jahamal came into view, I stormed past my mother and punched his ass in the face.

"Keifon! What are you doing? Stop!" My mother screamed as she rushed towards us.

Jahamal was trying his best not to hit me back, but I guess he got tired of me hitting him and pushed my ass back.

"What the fuck?" He yelled.

I advanced back towards him swinging, but he blocked it.

"Half my fucking life nigga."

"What the fuck you talking about, son?"

Not even my mothers cries stopped me from coming at him. I swing again as I yelled, "You killed my Daddy then got with my momma, nigga? You a grimy son of a bitch," I screamed.

I saw the moment that his demeanor softened. However, I didn't see regret behind his eyes, instead I saw that he didn't regret the shit at all. I saw admission. He was admitting silently that he did indeed do that shit.

"Keifon, please, baby," I heard my mother. I turned towards her with a scowl, causing her to look away. When she turned towards me she said, "It's wasn't like that."

"How the fuck is it then?" I hollered. Her eyes widened with a look of shock on her face. I have never disrespected my mother in that way. Never even raised my voice at her.

"Hold on now, you not about to be talking to your mother like that. You mad at me, fine, but don't try it nigga. I'm being lenient with your ass because of the circumstances, but don't try it."

"Nigga, I don't give a fuck what you got to say. Fuck you!" I hollered as I swung on him again. This time, he didn't hold back. We were fighting like hell in that living room while my mother screamed for us to stop. My mother didn't even attempt to break us apart, she couldn't if she wanted too. We were bangin' too hard.

"What the fuck is going on?" I heard Orion followed by him grabbing me pushing me back. I pushed his ass back trying to get back to Jahamal. We both looked like wild animals. Orion pushed me again as he shouted, "Fuck you doing, bro?"

"Did you know? Were you in on this shit too? Lying to me half my damn life. Hun nigga?"

Orion jerked his head back frowning as he asked, "Fuck you talking about?"

"You know, I know your ass knows. Your Daddy killed mine." I glared at Jahamal.

"Keifon, Baby." My momma touched my arm and I yanked away causing her to stumble back as I yelled.

"You lied to me momma. How could you marry the man that tore our family apart? You ain't no better than this nigga." I regretted what I said when I saw the look on her face. I couldn't think about that, though. I was angry and it wasn't anything that either of them could do about it.

"Didn't I tell your ass not to talk to my wife like that?" Jahamal stepped in his face continuing to say, "You need to listen to what the fuck she has to say."

I looked at my momma who was still crying as her body visibly shook. Then I turned towards Orion who had a dazed expression on his face, then to Jahamal. I had nothing to say to none of them. I mugged his ass in the face as I said, "I don't have to listen to shit, fuck you nigga!" I then turned storming out the door.

I heard Jahamal yell, "When you calm your ass down, you need to talk to your momma lil' nigga. Coming up in here like you running shit. I understand you're hurt, but you are wrong." I didn't even acknowledge what he was saying, I continued to walk my ass out that door. I was so livid right now that I didn't know what to do.

I got in my car and drove away. I felt like I was driving with nowhere to go. Somehow, I ended up at Jenday's house. I didn't want to see anybody but her. I stood knocking on her door, and when she opened it, she gasped as she asked, "What happened to you?" She pulled me in the house pulling the door shut. She pulled me into her bedroom, then bathroom. When I saw myself in the mirror, I understood her reaction. My face held blood on it from my busted lip. I also had a bruise on the side of my head.

She instructed me to sit on the toilet and I did. I had yet to say a word, I just stared straight ahead. She began cleaning up my face which burned a little, but considering the pain that I'm in right now, nothing could hurt me. I felt betrayed in this moment. When Jenday was finish cleaning my face, I pulled her between my legs by the back of her thighs. My head fell back as I gazed into her eyes. She grabbed a hold of my face and leaned down for a kiss.

"You want to talk about it?"

I simply shook my head as my forehead fell against her stomach and my shoulders shook. These were tears of pain. I can't believe that the only family that I have kept this from me my whole life. I can't even see what my father could have done to Jahamal to make him do something like that. By the time Jahamal had entered my life, it had been at least two years since my father had been killed. Now I was wondering how long my mother actually knew that nigga. I shook my head as Jenday stepped back pulling my shirt over my head. She then yanked at my hand before pushing my pants down, prompting me to step out of them. She led me to the bed and I laid down.

"Whenever you are ready, I'm here to talk." Jenday pecked my lips after she got in bed with me. That's why I loved her so much. She didn't nag me to find out what was wrong, she let me know that she would be there whenever I was ready to talk. That's more than any woman had every done. Jenday was for sure the woman for me. She hasn't let me down, and I don't see her doing it anytime soon.

I closed my eyes thinking about my family. I had nothing to say to them, and it was nothing that any of them could say to me to make me forgive them. Fuck it, I got Jenday, and her family.

Chapter 14

Orion

When Keifon stormed out of the house, I just stood there in disbelief. I was so stunned that I couldn't do or hear anything. Shit, all I heard was ringing in my ears.

My father killed Keifon's father. Was on repeat in my head. I can't even fathom how my brother feels right now. I didn't know none of this shit, but I can see how it looks from his point of view. I don't like the shit, but I completely understood.

Hearing Iris's cries brought me out of my daze. I slowly turned towards them seeing my father attempting to calm her down. His eyes found mine and I could see the truth. I didn't want too, but I asked anyway.

"Is it true?"

My father let Iris go, but still had his arm around her neck. He looked towards the ground and lifted his head as he replied, "Orion, son."

"Don't son me. Is it true?" I raised my voice.

"Don't raise your voice at me. You need to listen."

I stood with me feet shoulder width apart crossing my arms over my chest. I was waiting to hear what his ass had to say.

"It's not how it seems."

"Then how is it Pops. That nigga didn't spazz out for nothing. It's obvious that he found some shit out. You got my brother pissed at me and I didn't know a mutha fuckin' thing. Y'all pushed for us to be close, and we've been close for years, and now this. I love my fucking brother. Blood couldn't make us closer, now I may have lost the closest person to me because of something y'all have been keeping from us. What kind of shit is that?" I was on one right now. I began to pace as Iris pulled away from my Pops and ran upstairs. I knew she was hurt because of the way that I was speaking to them, but right now, I didn't give a fuck.

"You need to calm down, you are upsetting your mother."

I scoffed as I walked away and sat on the couch. I lowered my head into my hands and then lifted it up as I pulled my phone out of my pocket. I dialed Keifon's number and waited while the phone rang. Of course he didn't answer. I tried once more with the same results.

"Man, fuck," I hollered out as I stood. I had to find my damn brother.

"I have to get the fuck out of here."

"Orion, you not even going to let me explain?"

"I don't believe there is nothing to explain. You did what you did and fucked everything up. Keifon may never forgive us."

"Son wait, please."

I stopped with my hand on the door nob. Without turning around I said, "Nah, go on and check on your wife. Y'all deserve each other." I then walked out of the house leaving the door wide open.

I got in my truck and sat there for a few minutes thinking. This was some fucked up shit. I didn't want to think that my Pops and Iris were some grimy mutha fuckas, but it was looking that way. I kind of felt for the way I spoke to Iris. She has been nothing but a great mother figure to me all of these years. Still, this shit had me looking at her sideways.

I finally crank up my truck and backed out of the driveway. I drove straight to Keifon's place. I didn't see his car, but I still got out of my truck and used my key to enter his home. I searched the place and it didn't look like he had been there at all. At this point, I didn't know what to do.

I left and drove around until I ended up at Oba's house. She was off for the next three days, therefore, I knew she was home. I knocked on her door waiting on her to answer. When she did, she automatically knew that something was wrong.

She reached out and grabbed my hand pulling me into the house. Once she closed and locked the door she circled my waist with her arms placing the side of her face against my chest. The feel of her against my body calmed me down a little.

We stood that way for three minutes before she lifted her head so that she could see me. She lifted on her toes pecking my lips before asking, "What's wrong, babe?"

"Man." I raked my hand down my face before pulling away from her. I led her to the couch, sat down and pulled her into my lap. I rested my head against her shoulder and sighed.

"Shits all fucked up, Oba. That nigga Keifon just spazzed out on my Pops, his mom, and me. I had to break up a fight between he and my Pops. I don't know what to do at this point. He won't answer my calls."

Oba face scrunched up as she asked, "Well what happened?"

"Apparently, my Pops, killed his."

"Did you ask your Dad if it was true?"

I nodded my head as I replied, "He just said that it wasn't what I thought. I don't understand that and didn't stick around to hear it."

"Why is he mad at you?"

"Because he thinks I knew, but I didn't know shit. Had no idea, baby. I'm hurt that he would even think it. Keifon and I are close. Even though we don't have the same blood flowing through our veins, he is still my brother. On top of that, he is my best friend. I would never betray him that way. If I would have known, I would have told him that shit. I don't even know how he would have found out. Its like this shit came out of nowhere." I shook my head.

Oba was silent for a few seconds before saying, "Maybe you should hear your Dad out. If what was said was true, I don't see him just killing a man for no reason. What is Iris saying about it?"

I shrugged as I responded with, "She isn't really saying anything. She was so upset and hurt that she only cried. Then she just ran upstairs. I don't know man." I let my head fall back against the couch and closed my eyes. Oba and I sat in silence as I thought about this shit. When I lifted my head, I got my phone out of my pocket and tried to call my brother again. And again, he didn't answer. This shit was really tearing me up inside.

I pulled up my text messages and scrolled to his name.

Bro, I swear to God I didn't know nothing about that shit. I would never betray you like that. Please call me so we can get through this shit.

I waited a few minutes and he hadn't responded yet. I then sent another message.

Bro, they wrong as hell, but I HAD NOTHING TO DO WITH THIS SHIT! You are my brother and I love you. Call me back or I'm coming to look for you.

I sighed as I stared into Oba's eyes. She looked away then turned back saying, "Maybe you should hear them out?"

I frowned jerking my head back as I asked, "For what? Ain't nothing they can say to make me think anything other than their grimy. It seems like he killed Keifon's Dad and married his momma. This shit is all fucked up. Maybe I will hear them out, but not right now. I don't want to talk about this shit no more. I just want to be up under you until I leave to go find my brother."

She understood what I was saying and chose not to say anything else about it. I told her that I was hungry, and she got right up to cook me something to eat. That's why I love her little fine ass. She knew when to quit, and when to keep going.

Iris

I knew that one day this situation was going to blow up in my face. I kept a lot of things from Keifon when he was a child. His father loved him and treated him well. It was me that he treated like shit. I wasn't one of those mommas that put their child in the middle of their drama. I never spoke bad about his father in front of him. I was that momma that let the child figure things out on their own.

I was laying across the bed crying when I felt Jahamal enter the room. I knew it was him because I smelled his cologne. I felt the bed dip and he lay back beside me. I felt his arm around my waist as he gently pulled me on top of him. He engulfed me in his arms as he kissed my temple.

"It will be okay, baby."

"But how? Keifon was so damn mad. I have never seen him look at me, nor talk to me like that. Then Orion...I don't want to lose their respect, and that's what is happening."

He lifted my head and gazed intently into my eyes, "Do you trust me, baby?"

Tears were rolling down my face as I nodded my head. He then stated, "Then trust me when I say that I am going to fix this. I didn't do anything wrong. Tony's ass deserved everything he got. He was in the wrong, not me. All we have to do is get Keifon, and Orion to listen and they will understand why I had to do what I had to do. I got you, Iris."

I blew out a breath as he kissed my tears away. He had me hot right now even though I shouldn't be. I moved my hips back and forth feeling his monster dick rise. My husband was blessed in that department. I sat up removing my shirt, then stood and removed the rest of my clothes while he did the same thing.

I lay back on top of him crashing my lips into his. I tried to put his dick in my pussy, but he flipped me over and ate my pussy. My husband had my ass climbing the headboard.

"Stop all that moving."

"It feels so good," I moaned.

"Taste good, too."

He brought me to an earth-shattering orgasm before kissing up my body and entered me slowly. We both moaned as he made love to me. This wasn't going to fix the situation, but I damn sure felt good in this moment. I just prayed that my husband could fix this. Besides my husband, my sons are my life.

Chapter 15

Keifon

I've been at Jenday's house since yesterday. I didn't want to go home, because I knew that would be the first place they would look for me, and I wasn't ready to listen to them just yet. I needed time to process this shit.

I received every last one of Orion's messages, but I didn't want to talk to his ass either. My mind was going a mile a minute. I just kept thinking about how I felt as a child when my mother told me that my father had been killed. I knew he was in the streets because I wasn't a dummy. Since I knew what he was into, I never questioned my momma when she told me what happened. I never thought that it was all a lie. She knew that nigga Jahamal did that shit and still got with him.

It was past midnight and I was sitting on the porch smoking a blunt. This was the only way that I wouldn't go back over there and beat that niggas ass again. The front door opened causing me to look back. Keith stepped out on the porch and I went to put the blunt out.

"Nah, you don't have to do that for me. I see you are stressed. I'm good, trust me. In rehab, I learned that I am stronger than I thought."

He sat in the chair beside me as I asked, "You sure?"

"Yea, I'm good."

Keith and I have gotten close ever since he was in rehab. Jenday didn't know, but I was able to talk to the facility manager into letting me come visit him once a week. He wasn't supposed to have visitors, but I could be real persuasive. That bitch wanted to fuck, but I would never.

I sat there continuing to smoke as Keith asked, "You want to talk about it?"

I looked towards him for a few seconds before sliding my hand down my face. I took a pull of the blunt, letting the smoke out in front of me.

"Man, my momma and Jahamal did some fucked up shit. I just don't know what to think at this point."

He waited for me to continue, and I told him about who Puma was and what happened when I went to visit him. I could tell that he was uncomfortable with what I was telling him, however, I could also see that he wasn't judging me which I appreciated. He didn't say anything for a long while.

"You know, after meeting your Step Pops, I don't see him being grimy like that. I don't see him murdering anyone for no reason. Something had to have went down. When you were younger, do you remember anything that wasn't right in the house?"

I shook my head as I replied, "Nah, my father was my hero. He was there for me, spent time with me, all that."

"I will tell you this. When the girls mother and I had issues, we never let them know it. The only reason they knew something was going on was because I use to leave days at a time. It was even sometimes I would be sniffing that shit, and Jenday walked in. My daughter wasn't stupid so she knew shit wasn't right. But her mother never said anything. She spoke highly of me even though I didn't deserve that shit. I say all of that to let you know that something was probably going on in your house that you didn't know about. You should talk to your folks and let them explain why what went down happened. I can tell that y'all are a tight nit family and love each other. Just give them a chance."

I took a puff of my blunt letting the smoke fill my lungs. I let it out through my nose as I thought about everything that Keith was saying. I knew he was right, but it was still hard.

"I feel you, I think I just need time. I know I hurt my mother with my words, and I feel the worse about that. Then Jahamal..." I shook my head thinking.

"I put my hands on this man and he has been nothing but a great father to me ever since he came in my life. I think I fucked up, Keith."

He nodded as he replied, "Probably, but I'm sure both Iris, and Jahamal understands why you were mad. Once y'all get a chance to talk, things will be all good."

"I hope so man, I really do."

The front door opened again causing both Keith and I to glance back.

"Hey, I reached over and you weren't there," Jenday spoke in almost a whisper. I still haven't explained what happened, but knew I needed too.

"Yea, just needed to come out here and clear my head. Your Pops helped with that."

She smiled at her Pops before saying, "Alright. When you coming back to bed?"

I put the blunt out and replied, "Right now. Keith, I will see you in the morning. Thanks for the talk." Keith and I stood up and slapped hands before embracing each other.

"Good night, you two."

"Good night." I followed Jenday to the bedroom then closed and locked the door. She took her robe off before getting in bed. She held the covers back for me, and once I was unclothed, I joined her.

No words were spoken at first, but after laying there for a minute I told her why I was so upset. She let me talk for a long while without saying anything. Once I was finished, all she said was, "Things will work out." She kissed my lips then settled close to me and we soon fell asleep.

******

Like every other morning, I woke up to breakfast. This time, Jenday was standing there with a plate of, livermush, eggs, and roasted potatoes.

"Good morning, baby. Get up so you can eat."

I sat up swinging my legs off the bed before acknowledging her with a kiss, then moved to the bathroom to handle my business. I came back out and sat with my back against the headboard before reaching for my plate. I ate in silence as she watched. She was concerned, but she didn't have anything to worry about. I felt better than I did last night.

There was a knock at the door. Jenday went over to the window. She pulled the curtains back then turned towards me saying, "It's Jahamal."

I shook my head and said, "I'm not ready."

"Are you sure. I think you shou…"

"I said I'm not ready, damn!" I raised my voice a few octaves. I knew I shouldn't have, but I didn't need anybody telling me how I should handle this situation.

Jenday narrowed her eyes at me for a few seconds before walking out of the bedroom. I had already heard Jahamal in there asking Keith to come back here and get me. The next person I heard was Jenday telling him that I wasn't coming out and for him to try again another time. I then heard the door close.

I finished eating my food by myself. Jenday never came back into the room. In this moment, I didn't care, I wanted to be alone. I finished my food, sat the plate on the table and laid back down.

My phone beeped alerting me of a text message. It was Orion again. When I'm ready, he will be the first person I call. The more I thought about what Keith said, the more I didn't think he knew.

I tried to fall asleep but couldn't. I decided to get up and go on home. Jenday wasn't talking to me anyway. I got dressed and walked up front seeing Jenday sitting on the couch.

"Aye, I'm out."

She glanced back at my with her lips in a straight line. Yea, her ass was mad. All she said was, "M'kay." I stared at her for a second with her not even looking my way before leaving the house all together.

I pulled up to my place and then went inside. The first thing that I noticed was that my placed smelled like straight up weed. I didn't have to wonder who the hell was in my house, because only Orion had a key. I made my way into the living room seeing him sitting on the couch staring right at me. I continued moving through my place until I got to my bedroom. I took a shower, threw on some chill clothes, and then headed back into the living room.

I sat in front of Orion with my legs out, and one arm stretched against the back of the couch. We glared at each other not blinking once. Finally, he reached his blunt towards me. My eyes moved to it before I stood reaching over the table and grabbing it. I took a few puffs before I asked, "How long you been here?"

"I came that night, left, and I just got here about two hours ago."

I reached the blunt back to him, but he shook his head. I took the rest to the head before letting the roach drop in the ashtray. I guess neither of us had anything to say, because we were both silent.

"Look man."

"Bro." We both began to speak at the same time.

"Go ahead," I told him giving him the floor.

"Bro, I swear to God I didn't know anything about that shit. When you left the house, I cursed their asses out. It's one thing to do what Pops did, but they kept it from us all this time. Especially you. I didn't stay for long either. I felt bad when Ma ran upstairs. I just couldn't be around them at that moment."

I sighed as I raked my hand down my face and said, "I'm sorry bro. I shouldn't have acted like that towards you. I know you wouldn't do no shit like that. We have come a long way since we all moved in together. I was just mad as fuck at the time."

"I know you were. I would have been too. To think, they have been holding this in for all these years. If we feel bad, they feel even worse. I'm not going to sit here and demand that you talk to them, because I will be a hypocrite. However, I think that when you are ready, we both should go over there and at least hear them out."

I shook my head then thought about what Keith said. "Do you think some shit was going on in the house that I didn't know about, because Keith said it's possible that Ma, just didn't put me in her business."

Orion thought about it for a second and replied, "Anything is possible. It makes sense though. You know how Ma is. She never puts us in drama with her and Pops. Although we know every marriage has issues, we have never saw anything besides them loving on each other. Even when we were young."

"Yea you're right. We should go over there and see what the fuck they have to say, but I'm telling you now, if it's some bullshit, I am going to steal off on Pops. I'm still mad as hell, but at least I'm willing to listen."

Orion chuckled as he said, "You wild, but I can get with that."

"Alright, let me go throw on something, and I'll be ready." I stood up walking over to him holding out my hand. He stood reaching his out. We slapped hands, then hugged.

"I love you, nigga. You my brother and nothing will ever change that shit," I spoke sincerely.

"I love your ass too, bro." Just like that, we were back cool.

Orion

We listened to music as I cruised through the streets on the way to our parents house. Keifon reached up turning the music down. I could tell something was bothering him by the way he sighed and let his head fall back.

"What's up, bro?"

"Man, I think I fucked up with Jenday. I was so upset that I yelled at her. When I was leaving the house, she could barely look at me. I left without even apologizing. Man fuck."

I shook my head as I told him, "You need to fix that shit quick bro. Shit, you should have done that before leaving the house. After we straighten this shit out, I think you should holla at her."

"I will, I just need her to calm down."

"Don't wait to long, she might start to think you don't give a fuck. But honestly, you told her what you were going through right?"

Keifon nodded in response, and then I told me, "Then I'm sure she understands." He agreed with me just as I pulled my car in my parents' driveway. I asked Keifon if he was ready, and he took a few minutes before finally agreeing that he was ready.

We walked to the door together, side by side. I was with my brother with this shit. I am following his lead. Our parents owe both of us an explanation. The door opened and Jahamal stood tall in front of us both. Neither of us spoke a word. He stepped back allowing us to both walk in. I followed Keifon into the kitchen where we knew our mother was from the different smells in the air. She was cooking like she always did when she was upset.

There were all types of baked goods spread across the counter. She hadn't seen us yet, but when she asked, "Who was it, baby?" She turned stopping in her tracks. Tears built in her eye, but she didn't make a move to come to us like she normally did. Keifon sat at the table, and I followed his lead sitting beside him. Our mother pulled her pan out of the oven, turned the oven off, and then sat in front of us with our Pops beside her.

He reached over grabbing her hand communicating something with his eyes to her, that she seemed to understand by subtly nodding her head. She then turned her teary eyes towards Keifon and spoke lowly, "Keifon, I am sorry for keeping those awful things from you. You were young, and I felt like you didn't need to know what happened to your father in depth. Some things are better left unsaid."

"But how is the truth better left unsaid Ma?" Keifon calmly asked.

Ma shook her head before tears finally spilled over her eyes. She looked at our pops and he thumbed her tears away before saying, "Sweetheart, you got this. He needs to know the truth."

"You tell him?"

Our Pops disagreed by saying, "You have to start from the beginning, and only you can tell your story."

She grabbed his hand interlocking their fingers as she took a deep breath before her eyes fell to me, and then Keifon.

"Okay, when you were younger, Tony and I had a lot of issues. From the outside looking in, we were damn near perfect. However, anytime we were alone, he would put his hands on me."

"What!" Keifon shouted, even I was looking at Ma like she was crazy. It was obvious that neither one of us have heard this story before.

"Hold on a minute son, let her finish," our Pops stated and I could visibly see Keifon calming himself.

"Go ahead, sweetheart."

"Anytime you were home, Tony was the perfect man. But anytime you were at school, or out with your friends, that's when things went left. He treated me like shit, baby. I was so miserable with him. I use to use makeup to cover up my bruising, because I never wanted you to see me that way. I never wanted you to think bad about your father."

"But if you would have told me, I would have helped you Ma. I don't like this, father or not."

"That's the thing I was afraid of. I knew how you were about me, even at a young age. You would have done anything to protect me, and I didn't want you to get hurt. No matter what you would have done, he was older, and much bigger than you. I couldn't have him hurting you the same way he was hurting me."

Keifon lowered his head and wiped at his eyes. I knew he had tears in them because he loves his mother so much. I could see that this story was tearing him up since he wasn't able to do anything about it. He finally glanced up and motioned to our Pops with his head while asking, "Well, how did this nigga get in it?"

She looked at Jahamal, and that's when he started talking. "Tony and I sort of worked together. He would always come to work spitting that chauvinistic bullshit about how it was the woman's job to stay home and take care of the house. He boasted about how Iris did anything he asked, and when she didn't, he would beat her ass. Some of the men up there agreed with him, but others like me didn't agree at all. We were cool up until he came to work so angry. Someone asked him what was wrong and he said that Iris had left the house to hang with her friends and didn't have dinner ready the previous night.

Well that same morning, I knew you were at school, and I knew where you all stayed because I dropped Tony off one day when his car wouldn't start. I made up an excuse as to why I had to leave the shop and headed over to her home..." He paused for a second taking a moment to compose himself.

"As soon as Iris opened the door, it brought tears to my eyes. I was furious. Iris and I stood there for a minute until she fell into my arms crying. I don't know if you remember this Keifon, but at one point your mother stayed in her bedroom for like a week. Tony told you that she had the flu and didn't want you to catch it..."

"I remember that," Keifon expressed.

"From that day on, Iris and I became friends. I was in the process of starting my own company, and getting out of that business. Well, your mother and I spoke everyday when Tony wasn't home. One night, you spent the night with a friend. Iris locked herself in the bedroom and called me screaming for help. I could hear him yelling in the background and trying to break down the bedroom door. I told her to keep the door locked and she did.

He must have knocked the door down, because when I burst through the front door, he was standing over her with a gun pointed towards her. I made myself known and he pointed his gun towards me, while mine was on him. The way he looked at me, I could tell he was out of it. He asked me if I was sleeping with her, and I said no, which I wasn't at the time. Things went by quickly after that. He shot me in the shoulder, and I shot him in the chest. He died, I survived, and I do not regret a minute of it. Because of him, I was able to marry the woman of my dreams, whom I didn't know I needed."

The room was silent. The only thing that could be heard was everyone's sniffles. All four of us had tears in our eyes for varied reasons. I felt bad for Iris, she is the sweetest woman that I know.

"Ma..." Keifon got chocked up and he stood rounding the table lifting her out of her chair. He hugged her tight as she cried into his chest.

"I'm sorry Ma, I shouldn't have talked to you like that. I love you okay?" he pulled back so they were looking at each other. She nodded her head and he hugged her for a few more seconds before turning to our Pops. He also apologized to him. I then stood up and did the same with both of them.

"Out of curiosity, son. Who told you that shit?"

"Puma," Keifon replied.

Even I had to look at the side of his head with a frown. That was news to me, I forgot to even ask who told him that. Our Pops only nodded as he hummed. I knew that sound, he was going to see Puma.

"Now that we all understand each other, from now on, we talk shit out instead of coming to blows. Only reason I didn't go hard on you was because I knew you were upset."

"Whatever Pops, you know you can't keep up with me with your old ass," Keifon stated causing us all to chuckled. Just like that, we were a tight ass family again. My mother had cooked all these damn sweets, and she packed them up so we could take them with us.

Jahamal
The next day

Puma has lost his mutha fuckin' mind getting into family business that didn't have shit to do with him. The only reason he even knew about what I did, was because he saw Iris and I out one day. She was feeling down about lying to her son about what happened. I asked her to get dressed and I was going to take her to dinner.

By that time, Tony had already been dead for a month. But Puma had to see me for almost tearing my family apart. I love them and no one was going to do anything to divide us. I just need to know why the hell he even said anything about that shit. It has to be a reason, and I have a feeling of what it was. There was no need to bring none of that shit up over a decade later.

I pulled up to the shop stepping out of the car. Some of the men standing outside recognized me and spoke. I was then told to go on in. When Puma saw me, he had a smug grin on his face. See what I mean, this nigga is a straight up bitch.

"What's up old friend, have a seat?"

"I'd rather stand." I stood with my feet shoulder length apart with my arm crossed over my chest. I narrowed my eyes at him and questioned, "What the fuck is your problem? What was the purpose, nigga?" I asked him. There was no reason to expound on what I meant because judging from the way he smirked at me, he knew exactly what I was talking about.

"What you mean, Jahamal?"

"Cut the bullshit, Puma. You knew what the nigga was doing to his wife. You knew he deserved that shit. Now you bringing my son into this shit. What the fuck for?" I had leaned over the desk getting in his face.

Puma sat back in his chair then said, "You're right. I knew if he went to you, that you would come to me."

"That makes no damn sense Puma. You have my fucking number. You could have just called me. But see, now you fucking with my family. You see what I did when I didn't even know my wife. Imagine what I would do now for fucking with her peace." I wasn't playing with his ass either. I'm mad as hell. He was taking me out of character. I've been on the straight and narrow for years, and it will not end well for him. He can think just because I went legit that I'm a punk if he wanted too. That would be a mistake on his part.

"You must have forgotten who I am," Puma stated causing me to jerk my head back.

"Nah, you must have forgotten who the fuck I am. You have me here, tell me what you want."

"I need you to talk to your boys about continuing this venture with me. Both of them are the truth. Besides that one mishap, I haven't had any other problems out of them. They only have one more car left to get for me, but I need them to continue doing their thing, and you are going to help me convince them."

I cocked my head to the side before laughing so hard my shoulders shook. Yea, he was out of his mind

"Look Puma, my boys are grown ass men. I can't make them do shit, and I am not going to try. And there ain't shit you can do about it."

Puma stood to his feet and rounded his desk which prompted me to stand to my full potential. He glared at me with narrowed eyes. The vein in his neck was protruding. He was mad, but I was furious.

"You are going to do what the fuck I say or that little family of yours is going to be no more."

"Nigga what?" I pushed his ass back and continued with, "You threatening me? Lets not act like I'm not as deadly with a gun as you are. Stay the fuck away from my family, or you will be in the ground with Tony's ass." With that I back up to the door. He didn't say anything, he just had that stupid smile on his face. I didn't put my back to him until I was fully out the door.

    This man was trying me for real. If he so much as says a word to my family, he will regret it. I am fully prepared to protect them by any means necessary. If it were up to me, Keifon, and Orion wouldn't finish this last job. But I wouldn't stop their money, I am just going to keep an eye out on Puma's bitch ass.

Chapter 16

Jenday

"I appreciate you Jenday, you always come through with this dancing shit," Bizo stated. I did yet another video for him. I wasn't going to come because I didn't want to see Keifon. But turns out, he didn't come anyway, which was perfect.

"No problem. You know I love to dance."

"Alright, Keifon treating you right?"

"Hmm." I rolled my eyes.

"Ahh hell. Y'all will be straight. You were made for him, baby. Whatever he did, give him another chance. I haven't seen my boy open up like he does with you. Be easy." He walked away.

I made my way to my car to head home. I hear what Bizo was saying, and believe it's true. We do make a great couple, I just didn't like the way he spoke to me, especially when I was only trying to help.

I think his situation is sad, but I needed him to get the full story instead of jumping to conclusions. Jahamal is a great man and have been there for Keifon, and Iris for a long time. I mean, he married her. So whatever his father did, had to be bad for Jahamal to feel like he had to protect Iris from him. I guess I think differently. I was always taught to always keep an open mind.

As soon as I pulled on my street, I saw his truck sitting there. I rolled my eyes as I parked beside him. I gathered my things and got out of the car. I wasn't going to say anything to him until he said, "You don't see me?"

I rolled my eyes and over my shoulder said, "I see you just fine." I searched for my house key on my key ring and was about to slide it into the keyhole when I felt his hand on my waist.

"Hol' up, baby. Can I talk to you for a minute?"

I turned around and was mad at myself for having impure thoughts. I was upset with him, but he was just so damn fine. *Damn.*

My right eyebrow raised and I cocked my head to the side as I asked, "Talk or yell?"

He raked his hand down his face and replied, "Jenday, baby. I am sorry for getting an attitude with you. It's just that I didn't know what to do with the information that I received. I shouldn't have yelled at you."

I looked off to the side before focusing my gaze back on him. My eyes misted as I said, "I just want the best for you. I don't want you to lose your family. You love them too much."

He pulled me close to him as he responded with, "I know and I realize that. I will never take my problems out on you again." He slid my bag off my shoulder, then grabbed my hand leading me over to the chairs on the porch. He sat down, and pulled me onto his lap encasing me in his arms.

We were silent for a long time before he asked, "Do you forgive me, Jenday?"

"As long as you promise not to do that shit again."

"I promise, woman."

I smiled and leaned in placing my lips against his. He pulled my body closer to his and we kissed passionately. I moaned into his mouth deepening it by gripping the back of his neck. I pulled away first gazing into his eyes.

"I love you, Keifon."

"I love your fine ass, too." He rubbed his hands up and down my arms.

"You're cold, baby. Lets get inside."

I stood up, followed by him. He grabbed my bag as I opened the front door. Of course Leah was on the couch like always. She looked back smiling as she said, "Hey, I was about to call you."

"I'm okay, sis. I've been here a few minutes talking to Keifon outside."

Leah lifted the remote turning the TV off as she spoke, "Okay, you know I can't sleep until you're home." She hugged me, then gave Keifon a side hug before disappearing down the hall to her bedroom.

"That's so sweet how she worries about you."

"Yea, it is. Come on." I led him to my bedroom. After locking the door, I came up out my clothes to shower. Keifon was right behind me. I had multiple orgasm's in the shower before we settled in bed for the rest of the night.

I lay my head on his shoulder as I rubbed on his stomach. He kissed my forehead before saying, "I had a sit down with my family."

I smiled as I replied, "That's good. What did Jahamal and your mom say."

"Well first, when I left your house, Orion was at mine. He didn't know and was as upset as me. We made up and then went to our folks house. Apparently, my Dad was a bad man. He used to beat my mother. He and Jahamal worked for the same man. The same man that Orion and I are involved with." I listened intently to Keifon telling me the story he was told.

"So yea, that nigga use to brag about putting his hands on my momma. When that shit happened, Jahamal walked in on my mother on the floor with Tony standing over her with a gun. Her face was swollen and blood covered it. Jahamal got shot in the shoulder, and he killed Tony. He wasn't charged because it was obvious what was going on."

"Damn. I'm glad she made it through. She didn't deserve that just because of the way he thought life should be."

"I'm glad that nigga dead, or I would have done it myself."

"So y'all good now?"

"Yup. We made up and shit," he replied.

"Good baby." We lay there in each others arms until we fell asleep.

Oba

"That food was good as hell," I said to Orion. We were leaving the newest restaurant in Charlotte, Steak 48. Those steaks were so juicy and tender. It was hard to get into that place, but Orion had connections that got us in.

"Yea, it was. You tryna go home?"

"As long as I'm with you, it doesn't matter."

He leaned in pecking my lips as he opened his car door allowing me to get in. He closed the door, then rounded the back before getting in.

We drove listening to old school R&B. In no time, we were pulling up to the lake in University. It was fall, but nice outside. He got out the car, then helped me out. He held my hand as we walked through the shops to get to the lake.

"It's always beautiful out here."

"Not as beautiful as you, bae." I smiled as he put his arm around my waist.

"You're just saying that because you have too."

"Nah, that's real shit, baby. I love everything about you. That's why when you first walked into my hospital room, I had to get at you. Shot up and everything. I wasn't letting your fine ass get away."

Oh he was laying it on thick, and I had nothing to say besides, "Yea, you were going kind of hard acting all thirsty."

"Shit, I was dehydrated as fuck." We both laughed. We came to a low brick wall and he lifted me up sitting me on top of it and standing between my legs. I was all smiles, Orion was forever wanting to spend quality time with me. This was something that Tommy rarely did.

Orion's phone rang and he removed it from his pocket. He looked at it saying, "Hold on, baby. This is Paul. Hello." He put the phone on speaker.

"What's good man?"

"Shit, sitting here spending time with my baby."

"Oh, hey sis."

"Hey Paul."

"Good, I have both of you here. I heard from my buddy downtown. This nigga Tommy played like he was crazy in the hospital. I heard he was screaming at you, Oba. When he left to be transported to jail, they said this nigga was acting psychotic. Because of that, they sent him upstairs to be put on a psych hold instead of arresting him. He even acted crazy up there. Had to sedate him several times. I say all this to say, my buddy thinks he is going to be committed for reasons of insanity. He won't go to jail."

"What?" I hollered pissed as hell.

"That fool is not crazy."

"Yea I know. My buddy doesn't think so either. He tryna play the system." I could only shake my head as they continued their conversation.

Orion hung up the phone as he sighed. I pushed out a breath and said, "He is trying to get back to me. I can feel it."

"He ain't going to touch you. He'll be in the ground before he blinks."

I didn't say anything. I believed Orion, but what about when he isn't with me? He must have read my mind because he said, "I will protect you at all cost. Even if I have to take you every fucking where. Paul said one thing that was true. He is crazy, but not for that reason. He is crazy for thinking he can come at you without consequences."

I placed my arms around his neck pecking his lips a few times. We hugged before pulling away. We stayed out there for an hour before heading back to the car so we could go to my house.

At home, we showered then I put on a pair of panties, and a tank top. I stood to go get me something to drink.

"Got damn. Look at all that ass." He squeezed my butt causing me to giggle.

"I don't think you know what you got back there. Mmm mmm mmm," he let out.

"Boy, you crazy. You want something to drink?"

"Bring me one of those Dr. Peppers you got in there."

"Okay." I walked out of the room and came right back."

"Here you go, babe." I handed the bottle to him and then sat on the bed.

We had been watching, Outer Banks, on Netflix for the past few nights, and he had it ready to go. He pressed play and I snuggled close to him. His hand stayed on my ass like he was addicted. I had no complaints though.

"Babe, if you keep rubbing on my ass, we not going to be watching TV."

"Shit, we can pause this shit. Matter of fact…." He paused the movie and tugged at my panties until I lifted up so that he could take them off. Next was my shirt, then his clothes. He settled with his face between my legs and needless to say, we didn't watch shit.

Chapter 17

Three days later

Jenday

"Girl, I'm glad they invited us down here. I haven't been on a good shopping trip in a while," Oba stated as we were walking out of Peachtree Mall in Atlanta. We had so many bags filled with items that Keifon and Orion gave us money to buy. They handed us so much money that we still had a few thousand left in our purses.

"Where you trying to go now?" We still have a few hours left before they returned to the hotel. I have been praying the whole way that they returned safely to us.

"We can go eat. You want to try Kandi's restaurant, Ol' Lady Gang?"

"Yea, we can do that," I replied.

We got in the car and headed that way. We had to wait thirty minutes to be seated. We looked over the menu and gave the waitress our food and drink orders.

We were almost done eating when I happened to look up at the TV on the wall. My eyes ballooned as I whispered, "Oh my God. We have to go." I abruptly stood as I reached in my purse pulling out a hundred dollars and threw it on the table.

"What's wrong?" Oba was staring at me like I was crazy.

"No time. Lets go!" I bolted towards the door. Oba better bring her ass or she was getting left. I ran all the way down the street to the car and got in cranking it up. I played with my phone trying to get the live footage of the police chase that was happening.

Oba finally got in the car all out of breath. Shit, I couldn't breath either, but I had to find out their location. No way in hell was I letting my man go to jail.

"Tell me what's wrong, Jenday. Do you know those people on the TV."

I glanced at her before putting my car in drive and pulling off. I could feel her staring and finally replied, "It's Keifon and Orion."

"What? What you mean? They don't steal cars." I glanced at her, my lips in a straight line then focused back on the road. I came up with a plan. I just hoped it worked

"They brought us down here on some criminal activity shit?"

"Calm down. This their last one. Then their out. Here, call their phone." I handed her my phone.

"Baby, we are in trouble," Keifon said when he answered the phone

"I see it."

"If I don't make it out of this, just know I love you, and I'm sorry."

"No, you're going to make it out." I stayed as calm as possible.

"I don't know baby. We are far ahead of them but it's a matter of time before they block the roads of something."

"I have an idea. There is a parking deck three streets up from you." I ran down my plan and they agreed to do as I said. We stayed on the phone as I drove as fast as I could to my destination. I went to the third floor as I promised I would. I just hope they could run like hell.

"Jenday, what is going on?" Oba asked.

"Hush, I need to concentrate."

Oba smacked her teeth and sat back. I could hear the sirens, so I knew they were close. My heartrate sped up as the sirens got closer.

"Get in the back." Oba listened and got in the back and slid over leaving the back door open like I asked her too. I got in the passengers seat leaving the drivers side open. From the corner of my eyes, I saw the door open to the stairwell. Keifon hopped in the drivers seat, and Orion got in the back slamming the door.

"It worked." I hugged him kissing all over his face.

"I'm good, baby. Thank you. Now just stay calm. We are going to follow these cars out when I catch my breath. A nigga smoke too much for this shit," said Keifon.

I pulled my seatbelt on listening to Oba and Orion argue.

"What the fuck Orion? You putting my life in danger now?"

"Man, we good. I didn't put your life in danger. I just wanted you to enjoy the weekend. We didn't know this shit was going to happen," Orion replied to her.

Oba slammed her back into the seat with a huff not saying anything else.

"Man, bro, that shit was a set up. They knew we were there. What the hell? Do you think Puma did this shit?" Keifon asked.

"I don't know, but as soon as we get out this parking deck, I'm calling Jahamal."

The car was filled with silence as Keifon pulled out behind three other cars. When we got to the first floor, cars were lined up trying to get out. It looked like they were checking all the cars. We all looked straight ahead until it was our turn.

The officer flagged us down motioning for Keifon to roll down the window. Keifon did as he asked saying, "Good evening officer. What's going on?"

The officer ignored what he asked with his own question, "Good evening, did you all see anyone running up there or a suspicious car?"

Keifon played his roll by saying, "No sir, my wife and friends came from the restaurant off the third level. We didn't see anything out of the ordinary. Is it safe for us to leave, sir?"

The officer looked through the back window before focusing back on Keifon.

"Yes, we have Officers all around. If you just follow the other cars and turn left only. Have a great rest of your day."

"You too, sir." Keifon rolled up his window and pulled off."

I felt relieved as I'm sure everyone else in the car did. This was a crazy ass day, and I was ready to leave. The rest of the way to the hotel was silent.

******

We had adjourning rooms. Orion, and Oba went into theirs and we entered ours. Keifon opened the door that separated the rooms, and Orion was doing the same thing. When he turned around, I jumped into his arms holding him tight.

"That was a close one, please don't do that again. You have to stop."

"I know baby. Fuck that money, being in the free world with you and our families is more important. But go ahead and pack our things. We cutting this trip short."

"Okay." I replied as I let him go and did what he asked.

Orion

I glanced at Oba rocking back and forth on the bed. I knew she was scared because I could see her shaking.

"Baby..." I sat beside her.

She slowly turned her head towards me. I grabbed her hand saying, "I'm sorry. This was supposed to be our last car theft. I know that nigga set us up some kind of way. I will never put you in that type of situation again."

Tears welled in her eyes as she replied, "Why are you doing this? Does the club and gambling spot not make enough?"

I shook my head as I pushed air out of my mouth. I looked at her and told her, "It's not that. I was just trying to be set."

"I'm upset that you kept this from me, but at the same time, glad that you are okay. I didn't know what was going on when we seen that chase on the TV. Baby, I don't know what I would have done if..." she shook her head not finishing her sentence. I pulled her into my arms pecking her lips.

"I'm okay. We're okay. You don't have to worry about that shit anymore. I love you."

"I love you too, Orion." We kissed once more before I asked that she pack our things. We had to get up out of Atlanta. I stood up to open the balcony doors as I hollered, "Bro, come holla at me on the balcony," I said to Keifon.

He appeared a minute later with a blunt in hand. Yea, we needed that shit. My nerves were shot right now.

"Aye, you don't think Bizo was a part of this too, do you? He did cancel on us at the last minute. That should have been a sign." I inquired.

Keifon shook his head saying, "Nah, he wouldn't do no shit like that. He would run the risk of being implemented. Plus, we knew his manager set him up with a last-minute show. Let me call and let him know what's up." He pulled out his phone dialing Bizo as he asked, "What about Puma?"

"I'm not sure. But you know Pops talked to that nigga when that shit with your donor went down. I'm not sure what happened. But I'm calling him now." I lifted my phone dialing our Pops number. Bizo had answered and Keifon spoke to him as Pops answered the phone.

"Hello."

"Yo Pops. We were in a fucking high-speed chase. If it weren't for Jenday and Oba? We would be fucked right now. Dead or in jail."

"What the fuck happened?" He asked.

I ran down the story to him and he was cursing up a storm. "I knew that nigga was going to be a problem. I warned his ass. Now he is going to wish that he listened. Listen, I don't know what Puma has planned, but he threatened the family. When you get back, keep your eyes open, and watch your woman. He can't be trusted at this point. I got something for his ass though."

"Pops, don't try to get at him without us. Wait until we get back. Are you going to tell Ma?" I asked.

"I have to. There is no way I can keep this from her, especially when someone is gunning for us. Y'all just hit the road right now."

"Oh yea, Jenday and Oba are packing now. We leaving in the next ten minutes," Keifon spoke up when he hung up with Bizo.

"Okay, be careful. Love y'all."

"Love you too, Pops," Keifon and I replied simultaneously, and then I disconnected the call.

"This some straight up bullshit. Fuck Puma. What Bizo say?" I stood up heading inside, and Keifon was right behind me.

"He mad. He ready to handle him when we get back."

I nodded my head as I asked Oba, "We all set, baby?" I asked Oba. Her body was still tensed. She was worried, and I understood why. I don't think she will calm down until we are out of Atlanta. I feel her on that. She ain't never been through no shit like this.

She nodded her head as I wrapped my arms around her waist saying, "Listen, I know you haven't experienced anything like this before, but you handled yourself well. You could have folded and told it all when the officer was at our car, but you didn't. I owe you."

"I would have never done anything like that. I may not agree with that part of your life, but I love you and would never put your life in peril no matter what. But that shit scared the hell out of me, Orion. I've never been so scared in my damn life. But like you said, you are good. We are good, as long as you never do anything like that again. Your gambling spot is as far as illegal activity that you go. Even with that, we are going to work on making that shit legal." She held her head up high, confidence pouring from her as she put her foot down.

"Damn that shit was sexy as fuck. Tell me how it really is, babe."

"Aye, y'all ready?" Keifon stood at the adjourning doors and asked.

"Yea, lets get the fuck up out of here." I let Oba go and grabbed our bags.

******

It took us five hours to get back since we stopped to get something to eat once we were in South Carolina. After dropping Keifon and Jenday off at her house, where his car was parked, I drove over to Oba's house.

"Hey, I'm about to shower and wash this trip off me. You coming?" She was standing in front of me getting undressed.

My eyes raked down her thick ass body as I pulled my bottom lips into my mouth.

"Shiiit, you don't have to ask me that." I came up out of my clothes and joined her in the shower.

"You look stressed. Let me handle that for you." She lowered herself onto her knees and deep throated my dick.

"Damn." My back fell against the shower wall. That's how hard she was going. Felt like she was trying to suck my soul out my body.

"Fuuuck," I hollered as I held her head and thrust my hips forward as I let lose down her throat. Her eyes were on me as she smirked , standing up and wiping the corners of her mouth.

"Let me see."

She opened her mouth and there was no nut in sight. I pecked her lips before saying, "Bend that ass over and let me murder that pussy." She did what I asked, and I did exactly what I said I was going to do.

Chapter 18

A month later

Oba

"Hey Dola." I hugged my sister as I walked through her front door.

"Hey sis."

"Auntie," My nieces Cameron, and Christina sang as they ran towards me. I bent down hugging them. I glanced up seeing Michael walking down the stairs.

"Hey Aunt Oba."

"Hey Michael." He gave me a quick hug.

"Where is Paul?" I asked.

"Oh, he is on his way home from work." Dola led me into the kitchen where she was cooking dinner. It was early as hell, but she always cooked early to get it out of the way. If felt like it had been forever since I've seen any of them.

"Are you staying for dinner?" Dola asked me.

"Nah, I am going to the nail salon with Jenday and her sister."

"Aww, I wish I would have known, I would have cooked earlier. I wouldn't mind a little girl time."

"We will be sure to invite you next time," I replied.

We conversed for a while. I told her what Orion found out about Tommy and she was just as upset as I was. No one can believe that he played crazy to get out of jail time, then again, yes, we could.

Paul walked into the kitchen and gave me a hug before making his way to Dola. They shared a hug and kiss before he let her know that he was going upstairs to shower.

"I hope me and Orion are still going strong for years to come like y'all."

"I'm sure you will. Anyone can tell by the way you both love each other."

I smiled at her words just as my phone rang. It was Jenday letting me know that they were ready. I let Dola know that I was leaving then said goodbye to the kids before making my way to my car to pick up Jenday and Leah.

Jenday

"Hey girl," I spoke to Oba when Leah and I got inside my car.

"Hey Oba." Leah spoke as well as Oba put her seatbelt on.

"Hey y'all." Oba responded as she waved at my father who was standing at the door, then backed out of the driveway. She turned the radio on as she drove us to the nail salon.

Oba found a vacant parking space and then the three of us filed out of the car. We entered the shop and each of us was led by a nail tech to an available table.

"How is school going Leah?" Oba asked my sister.

"Great, I can't wait to start senior year."

"Oh, how exciting!" Oba expressed.

We continued to get our nails done, then got pedicures. After getting our eyebrows done, we paid for our services, and then made our way out of the nail salon.

"I enjoyed myself with you girls today. We have to get together more often. Plus, my sister wants to hang out next time," said Oba.

"We can do that. I don't have any friends, and I like hanging out with you, too," I replied.

"Hey Ms. Lady. Damn, you're fine." A guy stepped in front of us with his attention on me. I grabbed Leah's hand because I didn't know this man from a can of paint.

"Thank you, you have a wonderful day. We have to go," I said.

"Hold up now." He moved when I moved still blocking my way.

"Can I get your number, get to know you and shit?"

"I have a man," I replied with the roll of my eyes.

"That's cool. Your man don't have shit to do with me baby. I'm Puma." He smirked. I narrowed my eyes at him knowing that name. I glanced over at Oba, and I could tell that she recognized his name as well. At this point I was panicking and wanted to get away from this man.

Leah could feel that something was wrong because her body stiffened beside me.

"Yea, you must have heard my name from your man. Give him a message for me. They owe me one more car, and I will be compensated one way or another." He licked his lips as he touched my face. I jerked my head back smacking his hand away as I grit through clenched teeth, "Don't fucking touch me."

Puma laughed as he stated, "Be sure to let him know how easy it was to get to y'all." With that, he waked away.

"Oh my God, come on, lets go," I frantically said as we hurried to the car.

"Jenday, what the fuck?" Oba stated as her hands shook while she crank up her car and pulled off.

I lifted my phone and called Keifon.

"What's up, baby?" He answered.

"Keifon…" My chest heaved as I looked in the side mirror making sure we weren't being followed.

"What's wrong?"

"Where are you?"

"My folks house," he replied.

"Is Orion there too?"

"Yes. What's wrong babe? You have me worried."

"You should be. We on the way." I hung up the phone instructing Oba, "Go to their parents house."

"Jenday, what's going on? Who was that man. He was scary," Leah asked.

"A bad man. Don't worry. Keifon and Orion will handle it." The rest of the ride was silent.

Our men were waiting on the porch when we pulled up. They walked over to the car and as soon as we were out of it, Keifon hugged me while asking, "Now tell me what's going on?"

"Puma approached us?"

"What!?" He hollered as he glanced up and down the street before replying, "Lets get in the house." He placed his arm around me and gently grabbed Leah's hand.

Once inside, he called out to Jahamal. He came downstairs smiling as he spoke. That smile fell once he realized none of us looked pleasant.

"Is something wrong?" Jahamal asked.

"Yea, that punk ass nigga approached them," Orion let him know."

"Hun? Tell me everything." Jahamal stated.

I told them what happened starting with how he tried to holla at me first, then I gave them the message that Puma had for them.

"Yea, he has lost his damn mind. First, he tries to set y'all up because y'all want out. Now he approaching your women. Nah, it ain't going down like that." Jahamal paced the floor.

"Hey." Iris walked into the living room. She too noticed our faces and the way that her husband was tearing a hole in the floor. Jahamal caught her up then asked her to take Leah with her into the kitchen. When they were out of sight, Keifon asked, "Did he touch you?"

I immediately shook my head. Maybe I shook my head to hard because before I knew it, I was rushing to the downstairs bathroom and leaned over the toilet as I threw up.

"Oh my God. What's wrong with my sister?" Leah stood in the doorway as Keifon held my hair back allowing me to get it all out. The next voice I heard was Iris.

"Hey, give me a minute with her." Keifon and Leah stepped out of the bathroom respectfully as Iris wet a rag and handed it to me to clean my face.

"Jenday, is there something you want to tell me." She was smiling ear to ear. I had no idea what she was talking about so I shook my head slowly.

"Your breast seem firmer, and you're glowing."

"What are you saying?"

"You're pregnant," she whispered.

"Hun? No I'm not," I replied. I couldn't be pregnant at a time like this when someone is after us." Tears sprang to my eyes.

"Oh sweetie." She pulled me into a hug.

"It will be okay. My son would never allow anything to happen to you nor my grandchild. Get a test when you leave here and take it when you get home."

"Baby, what's wrong?" I looked up to see Keifon, Orion, Jahamal, Oba, and Leah standing in the doorway.

Iris gave me a comforting look urging me to tell him. I took a deep breath as I said, "I think I'm pregnant."

"What, yes! I am going to be an auntie," Leah stated happily. But I couldn't enjoy the moment because I was worried about the situation that we are in. Everyone standing at that door seemed happy.

Keifon stepped to me as Iris stepped back saying, "Come on y'all, let's give them a minute."

"Aye, why you crying? You don't want to have my baby?" He lifted me up sitting me on the bathroom counter and standing between my legs with his hands on my thighs.

"What? No, it's not that. How can I be excited about this when we have an unhinged man, threatening us. What if he catches me alone, and hurts me."

Keifon held the side of my face saying, "You are my heart, and carrying our precious cargo. No way in hell would I let him get close to you. I will protect you with my life." He pecked my lips. His words weren't doing much to comfort me. I was actually afraid. That man walked up to us like it was nothing. Obviously, he had been following us and we never realized it.

"I know you would, but in the back of my mind, I know you can't be with me every minute of the day. You have businesses and stuff."

"Fuck that shit. I am not leaving your side. My businesses are run by trustworthy people. I don't have to be there every night."

I gazed into his eyes before smiling placing my arms around his neck telling him how much I loved him before sliding my tongue into his mouth. He then closed and locked the bathroom door.

"What are you doing?"

"You are having a niggas baby, and that shit has me hard right now."

My eyes stretched wide as he pulled my pants down taking them off.

"Your family is in the other room."

"And." He unbuckled his pants. The next thing I knew he was sliding into my pussy. His thrust were slow. I wanted to holler so bad, but knew I couldn't. I enjoyed the ride until we both came. He pulled out, cleaned us up then helped me put my pants back on.

"You know that I don't know for sure right?"

"If my mother told you then it is true. But to be sure, we will stop somewhere and get a test." He sprayed air freshener as I agreed. We then left the bathroom joining the others.

"Is everything okay?" Jahamal asked.

"Yes," I replied.

"Alright, I will keep an eye on that nigga. We will discuss this at another time. Orion, you should go home with Oba, and Keifon take Jenday and Leah home. I will be in contact with y'all in a few days. Be sure to call Bizo to warn him."

We all said our goodbye's and left. Our first stop was Walgreens. As soon as we got home, I took the test. Leah told my father and everyone was waiting patiently for the results.

Three minutes later, I was walking out of the bathroom with a smile that I couldn't contain.

"I'm having a baby."

"Yes." Keifon rushed over to me. He lifted me off the ground and I hugged him tightly. Leah was jumping up and down and my father had a smile on his face. I was happy in this moment, I hope my happiness stayed intact.

Chapter 19

Jahamal

I had been watching Puma for a few days now. It was apparent that he had no idea. If he was going to be threatening people and shit, he should have been watching his back. His ass was too confident thinking no one could touch him. Well, his ass was getting touched tonight.

I suggested that everyone comes to my house since I knew for a fact that nigga didn't know where I laid my head. But just in case, I gave Keith a gun so that he could stay here to watch our women as my boys, Bizo, and I handled our business.

"Y'all ready?" I asked as I came downstairs.

"Yea." Keifon, and Orion hugged their women before we were out the door. It was silent as we prepared mentally to handle this nigga. It was almost one in the morning, and I knew he was still at his shop because this is the time that he counts his money.

"It should only be two other men there with him. I want Bizo and Orion to hang back for a second and search the property. Keifon and I are going to enter his office. Y'all come when the building is clear," I instructed.

"Got'cha."

"Okay."

"We got it," were their responses. I parked on the side of the building at the mechanic shop so my truck wouldn't be seen. The four of us grabbed our guns and quietly walked over to Puma's shop.

Bizo and Orion headed towards the front, while Keifon and I headed towards the back. There was a man out front and before I turned the corner, I saw his head exploded. No one heard the shot since we all had silencers attached to our guns.

"The fuck." I heard but didn't know what happened after that. I'm sure my boy and Bizo can handle themselves.

Keifon and I stood outside of Puma's office. I glanced back at Keifon who nodded his head silently informing me that he was ready.

"Aye Spruce, come here a minute," Puma called out. No one answered and he called his name again.

"Fuck this nigga doing?" He stood from his seat to go search for him. Puma was so busy counting money that he hadn't looked up at the screen that I knew was there which he had views of the perimeter of the building.

"He's not coming?" Puma heard me reaching for his gun in his drawer. Before he could reach it, I appeared and let off a shot to Puma's shoulder.

"Ahh fuck." He fell back in his chair holding his arm. Crimson red seeped through his fingers, and he winced in pain as his eyes moved to the four men standing in front of him. He chuckled at the fact that he was caught slipping.

"What did I tell you, Puma?"

Puma groaned as he attempted to sit up. "Fuck you, Jah."

"Nah, fuck you. I told your ass not to fuck with my family, and what did you do?" I asked a rhetorical question. I knew Puma wasn't going to answer me therefore, I continued with, "You did that shit anyway. Then you approached my future daughter-in-laws. Well, message received. Now look at you. You are about to die because my sons, and Bizo wanted to make better lives for themselves; live a legit life."

Puma wasn't going out like no punk, I could see it in his eyes. He mustered up all his energy to reach for his gun. His fingers didn't even get to touch the gun before his body jerked as all four of us lit his ass up.

"Bizo, grab the tape over there." Bizo did as I asked him to do.

"Shit, get all that money too. That's for all your pain and suffering," I continued. Just from looking at it, it had to be at least six-hundred thousand on the table and sitting on the edge of the money counter he was using. Keifon glanced around the room seeing a duffle bag. He hurriedly placed the money inside for them to split equally later, then we left the building through the back door.

"You boys straight?" I asked as I pulled off heading back to my house where everyone was at. They all replied that they were. The rest of the ride back was done in silence.

As soon as I parked my truck in the driveway, Bizo let them know that he was out. Keifon let him know that he could come get his money the next day. We then slapped hands with him and he left.

As soon as we walked through the door, our woman ran to us throwing their arms around our necks.

"Thank God you boys are okay," said Iris as she hugged me tightly. I placed a kiss to her lips saying, "was there any doubt?"

Iris side eyed me causing me to chuckle and reply, "Baby, you knew I was making it back to you. We're not done with this thing called life yet." I held her tightly.

Keifon kissed Jenday before pulling away saying, "Hey I'm here and it's okay. Y'all don't have to worry about his ass anymore." Jenday let out a sigh of relief.

"You ready to go?" Orion asked Oba. She nodded her head saying, "Yes, I'm ready to go to bed."

"You ready Dad and Leah?" Jenday asked. They nodded their heads but before they left, I thanked Keith for keeping watch. They all said their goodbye's to Iris and I before leaving our house.

Keifon

As Leah and Jenday walked into the house, I asked to speak with Keith alone. We stood outside until the front door was closed.

"What's going on man?" Keith questioned. I was standing there sweating bullets. I reached into my pocket pulling out a small box. Keith glanced down at it, but held no emotion on his face. That made me even more nervous.

"Ever since I found out that Jenday was pregnant. I have been thinking about the future. I love Jenday, Leah and you. Now, I don't want to marry her because she's pregnant, I want to marry her because I love her. Do you give me your blessing to give your daughter my last name?" I waited for him to answer. He took a long time to give me his answer and I was losing hope. I was thinking that after all the drama, he didn't want me around.

Keith finally smiled and said, "Of course. I see you love my daughter. Any man that will take a life to do so Is alright with me."

I felt relieved as he hugged me.

"Whew, you had me nervous for a minute."

We chuckled and Keith asked, "You about to do it now?"

I shook my head saying, "It's been a long night. I will wait until the morning."

"Okay son, lets get in here and get some sleep. I can't wait to see the look on my baby's face."

The next morning like always, we sat at the kitchen table eating the good ass breakfast that Leah cooked.

Keith kept glancing at me. I know he was wondering when I was going to pop the question. For some reason, I was nervous as hell. We were now done eating and I figured it was now or never.

I took a deep breath before standing to my feet. I stood behind Jenday and turned her chair around facing me. I guess the terrified look on my face set off alarms in her head.

"What's wrong, babe?"

I glanced at Keith and then Leah before my gaze fell back on Jenday.

"Babe, I love you so fucking much. You are my rib, my life, my soulmate. Ever since I met you, I knew you were going to change a niggas life. I need you like I need air to breath…" I reached into my pocket, pulled out the ring and lowered down onto one knee.

"Oh my God." Jenday squealed with her eyes misting as she waiting on me to continue.

"It would be an honor if you take my last name before we welcome our baby into this world." Yes, it was confirmed at a Doctors appointment yesterday that she was indeed pregnant.

Jenday turned towards her father and Leah who were all smiles. She asked, "You two knew about this?"

"I didn't, but I am so excited. I'm going to have a niece or nephew, and a new brother." Leah was excited indeed.

"He asked me last night," said Keith.

"Stop stalling baby. You going to be a nigga's wife or what?" I had a serious look on his face. There was no doubt in my mind that she was going to say yes, but still, my heart felt as if it were beating out of my chest.

"Yes baby, I will marry you." She fell forward into my arms. I held on tight as I assisted her with standing. We kissed passionately before I pulled away removing the princess cut four carat diamond ring from the box. I slid it on her finger then we kissed again as she and Leah cried and Keith clapped. Leah and Keith came over joining in on the hug.

"After all I've been through in my life, I am finally getting a happy ending. My Dad is clean, I have my sister, and now a baby and a future husband plus his family. I love all of you," Jenday expressed.

"We love you, too." We said as a group.

Epilogue

Oba

Two years later

"Good morning, my love." I smiled hearing his deep raspy morning voice.

"Good morning." I turned my head so that I could kiss Orion's lips. I'm laying in bed wrapped in my husband's arms as he rubbed my protruding belly while he pecked the nape of my neck. Orion and I found out six months ago right after I had our daughter Odessa, that I was pregnant again. Orion expressed how he wanted at least four kids and I would give my husband anything that he wanted. It's the least I can do because he spoils me rotten.

Right then, we heard our daughter crying through the baby monitor. I sighed because I was tired as hell. I was about to get up but Orion stated, "I got her, baby." He kissed my temple as I lay my head back on the pillow while Orion got up to go get our daughter from her bedroom.

Life has been great. I quit the hospital because I was tired of working in the ER. Plus, Orion let me know that I didn't have to work if I didn't want too. I now do PRN work meaning that I only take jobs when I want to. My husband was rich. He and Keifon's club is doing great. On top of that, their gambling spot was now legal. Jahamal helped them get all their licenses and everything. I am proud of my husband.

A few months ago, we found out that Tommy was actually sentenced to seven years in prison for attempted murder and possession of an illegal firearm. He tried that crazy shit, but while he was in the mental hospital, the therapist wasn't convinced. During his trial, the therapist took the stand and told the judge that

Tommy's actions were not genuine. She stated that he was trying too hard to act like he was crazy. The judge believed the therapist and decided that his claims for insanity were not warranted. That was great news to me.

Tommy wrote me a letter saying how he still loved me and wanted to be together when he got out. Orion was the one to check the mailbox that day. My husband drove straight to Salisbury to visit him. He got Tommy straight saying that we were married and he needed to stop all communications or he was going to have him handled before he could even be released from prison. I guess it worked because I haven't heard from him since. Thank God.

"What's wrong with Daddy's Princess? You hungry?" Orion walked back into the bedroom. I sat up with my back against the headboard releasing my left breast out of my night gown so that my daughter could eat.

I watched as my sexy as husband made his way towards me. He was shirtless in only a pair of boxer briefs. This man was everything.

He sat on the bed as he kissed our daughter on the cheek before handing her over to me. She immediately latched on for her breakfast. Orion let me know that he was going to make us something to eat and walked out of the room.

Right then, my phone rang. I reached over grabbing it from the nightstand before answering.

"Hey Jenday."

"Hey girl, what you up too?"

"Feeding Odessa. This girl can eat." We both giggled.

"You ready for today?"

"Yes, it's my babies first birthday. He has been fussy all morning. What time y'all heading over?"

"Probably about two."

"Okay girl, I will see you then." We hung up the phone just as Orion walked back into the room holding two plates of food. He sat beside me and fed me waffles, eggs, and bacon as I fed our daughter.

"You are so good to me, Orion. I am thankful for you." I smiled, and he smiled back saying, "You are my Queen, you deserve it." He leaned over for a kiss.

We finished eating and he took our plates back downstairs of our huge home. He allowed me to find the house, all he did was pay for it.

We put our daughter back to sleep before having adult time. I lay on my side in pure ecstasy as Orion stroked my insides. I turned my neck and we kissed passionately as sweat covered our bodies. He squeezed my breast as I moaned his name repeatedly.

"Shit, this pregnant pussy wet as fuck." I moaned in response as I pushed my ass back meeting his thrust. We came at the same time then he slowly pulled out and I turned around facing him.

"I love you so fucking much," Orion expressed as he pecked my lips.

"I love you more."

"Impossible," he stated as we continued to kiss. We lay in bed until it was time to get up, get dressed and head to Jenday's house.

My life has been perfect since we got all the nonfactors out of the way. The journey that we took to get here has been worth it. I wouldn't change any of it. Tommy acting a fool is what led me to Orion and I thank God everyday for bringing me my peace.

Jenday

"You good, baby?" Keifon walked into our bedroom with our six-month-old son, Kian.

"Yes, I'm good. Thank you for getting him so that I can get ready."

"You ain't even got to thank me for that, baby. That's what I am here for; to make life easier for you." He leaned down to kiss my lips. Kian started squirming and Keifon held him closer. He has been the perfect husband and father. Everything that he ever promised me, he has done. He purchased us this big ass house, and I now drive a BMW truck. I love my damn car, and my house even more. We had plenty of space to have more kids in the future. I told his ass that we need to take a break in between our second and third child, because we had number one and two back-to-back.

Today is our daughter, Jaylee's second birthday party. We had our backyard decked out. It wasn't really over the top. Just enough for the kids to enjoy themselves. We have two bounce houses, and a petting zoo. For our friends that have older kids, we have a gaming truck in our circular driveway. Not to mention the playground, and trampoline in our back yard. The kids are going to have a blast.

"Hey sis, the decorations and everything are up. Mrs. Iris, Mr. Jahamal, and Daddy helped me." Leah walked into my room to inform me.

"Thanks sis," I replied as she sat on my bed as I pulled my shirt over my head. We all had on matching shirts with Jaylee's picture on it, and our relationship to her was on the back.

I am proud of my sister. She had a rough childhood not having parent's or what not. But she now goes to Johnson C. Smith University. This is her sophomore year and she is majoring in Biology with a minor in dance. Leah is going to grow up to do remarkable things.

Once I was dressed, I headed downstairs just as Oba and Orion were walking through the door with their daughter and her protruding belly.

"Hey boo," she said to me while giving me a side hug.

"Hey Oba, hey bro." I spoke to the both of them.

"Look at my niece, she is so cute." I lifted Odessa out of Orion's arms. I gave her a hug and kiss on the cheek before handing her back.

More people showed up as we made our way to the backyard. There were several tables and chairs for our guest to sit. I sat down and Keifon walked over with Kian. He reached for me and I grabbed him. Jaylee walked over grabbing my leg. She was a jealous little girl. Anytime I was showing Kian too much attention in her eyes, she wanted some too.

"Hey pretty girl." I leaned down kissing her cheek. She smiled at me before turning to Keifon lifting her arms in the air for him to pick her up.

"Come on with your spoiled butt," Keifon said causing everyone to laugh.

"Leave my baby alone," I replied.

"Daddy's baby knows she is spoiled. Ain't that right Princess? It's the only way to be." Keifon sat in the chair beside me and then leaned over for a kiss.

"Aye, the food ready, y'all can go ahead and fix your plates," Jahamal shouted. The party was in full swing at this point. Everyone got up to fix their plates. Oba and I stayed seated while our husbands fixed ours.

"You okay baby girl? You need anything?" My father, Keith walked over and asked.

"I'm fine Daddy. Keifon is fixing me a plate. That's all I need right now." I giggled. Everybody knew that I loved food.

He smiled then leaned down kissing my cheek before walking away. I was so proud of my Dad. He was over two years clean. He haven't even thought about drugs. He has redeemed himself as our father, plus he is a wonderful grandfather. He spoils my kids more than Keifon and I.

He still works for Jahamal's Security Company. He fit right in with the rest of the guys. He still lives in our childhood home and Leah stays with him sometimes when she doesn't feel like staying on campus. Our relationship with him is now stronger than ever.

"Girl, did you ever think we would be living this life? With husbands and children?" Oba rubbed her protruding belly.

"I can now," I replied with a smile on my face. I found myself happier than ever these days. Keifon and my children were the reasons for that.

Everyone was having a great time. After we finished eating, the kids went back to play. Kian was getting fussy so Iris took him up to his room to put him down for a nap. When she came back down, it was time to cut the cake. Everyone stood around singing, "Happy Birthday to you? Happy birthday to you, happy birthday to Jaylee, happy birthday to you. How old are you…"

I glanced around at all my friends and family. I stood beside my husband with his arm around my neck while he held Jaylee in his other arm. In this moment, my soul was full.

Keifon gifted me with a dance studio for my wedding gift. I now have my own dance studio where I teach low-income kids how to dance. I want them to be able to have the future that they want without their parents worrying about kicking out a lot of money for dance classes. I even have a competition team who has been on a winning streak for the past six months.. Life was great.

"Blow out the candles, Princess." Keifon urged Jaylee. Jaylee blew and we helped her out before everyone started clapping. This was the life I always wanted. Any man in the past were place holders until I met the man that I was meant to fall in love with. Keifon was that man, I finally got my happily ever after.

#TheEnd

Note From the Author

Thank you for taking the time to read my book. You are awesome. I would love to get feedback from each of you. If you could leave a review on Amazon or Goodreads, I would greatly appreciate it.

I love connecting with my readers, you can connect with me by following these pages…

- Quisha Dynae's Lit Lounge
- author_quishadynae
- @quishadynae
- quishadynaebooks@gmail.com

You can also find my catalogue on Amazon.com
Email me for paperbacks

Text **QUISHA** to **22828** for future releases, updates, and sneak peeks…

Other Books by Quisha Dynae

-Love the way you Lie

-Not Gon' Cry

-Side Nigga

-Sydney Valentine

-Loving you Hurts me

-A Hustla's Promise

-A Hustla's Vow

-Loving me Unconditionally: A Boss B*tch Love Story

-Loving a Thug on Valentine's Day

-His Essence Her Peace

-Entangled in his Hood Love 1-2

-Bad Boys Ain't no Good: Good Boys Ain't no Fun

-Captivated by a Queen City Killa

-She Fell For a F*ck Boy

-Loving him Through it all: Yancey and Ariel

-Selfish With Your Love

-Seasons of Love: Summer's Story

-Seasons of Love: Autumn's Story

-Seasons of Love: Wynter's Story

-Hittin' Licks: Forever his Rider

-instaGASM: An Erotic Novella

-instaGASM 2: An Erotic Novella: Zavion and Rita

-Unexpected Love

-Dope Love

-Traded a Lame for a Boss

-Traded a Lame for a Boss 2

Made in the USA
Columbia, SC
18 June 2024